I PUT A SPELL ON YOU

Also by Adam Selzer

How to Get Suspended and Influence People

Pirates of the Retail Wasteland

I PUT A SPELL ON YOU

FROM THE FILES OF CHRISSIE WOODWARD, SPELLING BEE DETECTIVE

DELACORTE PRESS

Published by Delacorte Press
an imprint of Random House Children's Books
a division of Random House, Inc.
New York

Delacorte Press and colophon are registered trademarks of
Random House, Inc.

Visit us on the Web! www.randomhouse.com/kids

Educators and librarians, for a variety of teaching tools, visit us at
www.randomhouse.com/teachers

Library of Congress Cataloging-in-Publication Data is
available upon request.
ISBN: 978-0-385-73504-9 (trade)
ISBN: 978-0-385-90498-8 (lib. bdg.)

The text of this book is set in 12-point Goudy.

Book design by Kenny Holcomb

Printed in the United States of America

10 9 8 7 6 5 4 3 2

First Edition

For
**Bob Woodward, Carl Bernstein, and Mark Felt—
American heroes**

From: Chrissie Woodward, former hall monitor

Re: the bee

Dear Esteemed Members of the School Board:

You stink.

Seriously. You really, really stink.

People should have been fired the morning after the all-school spelling bee. It's been a whole week now, and NOT ONE PERSON has been fired! No one has even been suspended!

I KNOW that you're not afraid to fire people. Remember Mr. Agnew, the old janitor? You fired him the very next day after that whole thing with the hamster and the cheese. The very next day! But it's already taken you over a week to fire people over a spelling bee that turned into a riot? Are you people nuts?

Well, of course you are. In addition to stinking, you're probably also nuts. If there's one thing I've learned from this whole business with the bee, it's that this whole *town* is nuts. It was just a spelling bee, people! Get a grip!

I've learned other things, too, though. Things about myself. And how wrong I was to

1

think that the people in charge always had my best interests in mind.

Up until about two weeks ago, I was the best hall monitor Gordon Liddy Community School ever had. I know everything about everyone in school, and I've ratted on plenty of kids over the years. I always thought that the people in charge cared about law and order, and that they only wanted us to get a good education.

That seems pretty funny to me now, though, because they totally didn't. I can't believe how wrong I was!

When the weekend after the bee passed and you hadn't fired anyone yet, I started to think that maybe, just maybe, it was because you didn't think you had all of the facts about what happened, not just because you stink. If that's the case, well, I'm going to help you out.

I'm probably the only person in town who knows the whole story of the bee.

But even I can't tell you the whole story myself. I've taken depositions and collected evidence from several of the key players, and the results of my investigation are in the following pages. These should help you understand exactly what happened and who the real crooks are.

The days when I assumed that you, the

people in charge, would do the right thing
are long over. But I sure *hope* you do.

I learned a lot of important lessons.
You can, too. You'd better, in fact.

Read these pages, and get on with the
firing!

C.W.

P.S. The following pages are for YOUR
EYES ONLY!

1
JENNIFER

myxomatosis—noun. A disease only rabbits get. *Even though she studied rabbits for a living, Samantha was not exactly sure how to spell "myxomatosis," and didn't particularly care.*

You might think this is weird, Chrissie, but I love it when snow gets into my shoes and my ankles get so cold that they actually hurt. Everyone knows that there's no feeling in the world better than taking off cold, snowy socks and putting on something warm, right? Well, you can't get that feeling if you don't get snow in your shoes in the first place. So when I walk home from school, I step in every snowdrift I see. Sometimes I just shove the snow right into my socks when I get close to home.

Does that seem too weird? I know I'm a *little* weird, but most of the people in this town are completely nuts. There's a difference, you know. And I'm not really sure which one of the two I am sometimes.

Anyway, you wanted my story from the beginning, right? That's where it starts. Walking through the snow. I was walking home last Monday, and I heard Marianne Cleaver coming up behind me.

"Jennnn-i-ffffeerrrrr!" she shouted.

She was hopping around, trying to step in the footsteps everyone else had already left, making her braids flop about like they were snakes attached to her head. It's a safe bet that she's never had a single snowflake get into her shoes. If you ask me, Marianne is a remarkably boring person.

If you gave me a choice between talking to her and having a bunch of bowling balls dropped on my toes, I'd have to think long and hard about which to choose. If I were any meaner, I would have just run away, or maybe creamed her with some fresh snow, but I paused and waited for her to catch up with me.

"Hi, Marianne," I said, as politely as I could.

"I have to talk to you!" she said.

Well, that's just super, I thought. I assumed that she probably wanted me to join some new after-school activity she was starting—and that my parents would make me join, no matter how stupid it was. They're always looking for new ways to pad my college application, even though I won't be applying to any colleges for at least five more years. With all my activities, I'm lucky to get twenty free minutes per night.

"What's up?" I asked.

"Are you going to enter?" she asked.

"Enter what?" I asked, pretending not to know.

"The *bee*," said Marianne, as though she were talking to a five-year-old. "Are you entering? A, yes, B, no, or C, undecided."

Have you ever heard of people who read so many old

6

books about knights that it sort of gets into their head, and they start putting bowls on their heads and running around thinking that they're knights themselves? Well, Marianne is like that with tests.

She takes a practice SAT every night. Most of the books she reads in class during sustained silent reading (SSR) are books on test-taking skills. And somewhere along the line, she started thinking she WAS a test, or her brain got stuck in testing mode, or something like that. Whatever it is, it makes her speak in multiple-choice questions. It's like I was just saying—I may be weird, but I'm pretty sure she's nuts. She's always going around saying that she's "gifted," but I think that if I had whatever gift she has, I'd want to exchange it.

"C," I said, "undecided."

I jumped a step ahead of her to slide across a patch of smooth ice on the sidewalk in front of somebody's driveway. I'm an expert ice slider.

"But you did better than anyone else in our grade last year," said Marianne. "That makes you a prime contender."

"I guess so," I said. "What's it to you?"

"Well, isn't it obvious?" asked Marianne. "I need to know what the competition is going to be like, and I thought you might chicken out. So are you entering? You can't be undecided. Just A, yes, or B, no."

"I don't think I'll enter," I said, casually.

I actually knew perfectly well that I'd be entering. I just wanted to see how she'd react if I said I wasn't. It's fun to push Marianne's buttons sometimes.

"Can you tell me why not in fifty words or less?"

I stopped spinning for a second and wondered if Marianne was actually going to count how many words I used. I wouldn't have been surprised.

"Well, I won't be able to study much with all my other activities, for one thing."

My parents make me join *everything*. I was a member of the School Spirit Squad, secretary of the Recycling Club, and even the founder, and sole member, of the Flying Mermaids, the Gordon Liddy Community School synchronized swimming team. And on afternoons when the school doesn't have an activity or two to keep me occupied, they find other places for me to go. Until the school golf club and indoor soccer started to take up too much time, they'd signed me up as a volunteer bedpan cleaner at the nursing home. Yuck.

I don't even learn anything from most of them—most of them just take up time when I could actually be *learning* something. Honestly, sitting around eating cat food would be a better way to spend time than most of the activities, if you ask me. All I do in most of them is sit around while everyone else gossips about the people who aren't there.

But according to my parents, having an impressive college application is more important than actually being smart. I really hope they're wrong. I know for a fact that they're completely nuts, and people who are nuts tend to be wrong a lot, right?

But Marianne's parents believe the same thing, and she agrees with them completely.

"That's your excuse?" she asked. "Your activities are going to make you too busy to study?"

"That's my story, and I'm sticking to it," I said.

"Well, that's stupid!" she huffed. "I'm in just as many clubs as you are, and I'm president of four of them. But you can bet I'm entering!"

"When will you have time to study?" I asked.

"Simple," Marianne said. "I'm going to stop taking practice SATs and work on spelling exclusively. I've already read the dictionary five times. Now I'm going to *memorize* it."

I snorted. "The bee is next Friday. I think it takes longer than that to memorize the entire dictionary."

"I have a photographic memory!" Marianne said, lying through her teeth. "Even if you do enter, you're never going to win with talk like that!"

"What does it matter if you come in first, anyway?" I asked. "You don't need to win the whole thing to go to districts. You just have to be in the top five."

"Oh, puh-lease!" said Marianne. "Do you think colleges want to see 'All-School Spelling Bee Runner-Up' on the applications? No! They want champions!"

I hopped ahead to slide across another bit of ice—a rough, bumpy patch. Those are harder to move across—the trick is to put one foot in front of the other, then use the back foot to push yourself forward, and the front foot for steering and balance.

"Did it ever occur to you," I asked, "that maybe there's more to being a champion than just sitting around memorizing the dictionary all night? Like, if you have to give up your whole life to be able to win, you're not really the champion at all?"

Marianne chuckled. "That," she said, with this superior air that she gets now and then, "is loser talk."

I don't believe in violence, but I must admit that there are times when I'd really, really like to smack Marianne Cleaver upside the head. As it was, I just stared at her and hoped that if I concentrated hard enough on her head exploding, it might actually happen. It didn't, of course, but it never hurts to try.

I knew I'd be entering anyway. In fact, it DID matter to me whether or not I won, because my parents totally expected me to. It was an order. My sister, Val, won it three years in a row—she's the only fourth grader ever to win, you know. And I was nervous as heck about it. I didn't even make it to districts in fourth or fifth grade, and Val came in first when she was in both of those grades. After hours and hours of studying, my brain just froze up at the bee the last two years, I guess. That can happen, you know. You work your brain too hard, and it sort of melts.

I had a secret plan that I'd been working on for weeks. It was a new kind of studying that I thought might work better. Instead of just studying spelling, I'd be studying Shakespeare, the thing I like to study most. You can learn a ton of stuff from Shakespeare, you know. Stuff about history, language, human nature . . . I mean, EVERYTHING is in Shakespeare. I'd pick up plenty about spelling along the way, and maybe my brain wouldn't be melted by Bee Day this year.

It would be, like, Zen studying. Studying without studying. The None of the Above school of studying. Or something like that. All I had to do was try to get out of as many activities as possible so I'd have time to do it. And if it worked, maybe I could write a book on None of the

Above studying skills. Marianne would probably read it during SSR.

I wasn't sure what would happen if I didn't win. Most likely, I'd be signed up for ten more activities and find myself cleaning another hundred bedpans a week. But there was always a chance it would be worse. Dad went to military school for a couple of years when he was my age, and he always said that if I went, it would look better on my college application than all of the activities put together. I could see him saying I needed to go if I didn't win the bee, or I'd never get into business school and run a corporation when I grew up.

But I don't want to go to business school at all. I probably won't have to guts to tell him this until I'm eighteen, but I don't want to run a corporation, either. I want to be a hippie.

I saw a documentary about hippies on TV last year. They were these people back in the 1960s who wore brightly colored clothes and spent all their time playing guitars and dancing around in the woods. They didn't care much at all for money or careers—just helping make the world a better place. That's the life for me.

I asked my dad if there were still any hippies around, and he said that there were—in fact, he said, he'd just had to sit next to a couple of "smelly hippies" on an airplane. I'm pretty sure you can be a hippie without smelling bad. Or taking drugs, which Dad said the ones on the plane did. Or living in the woods all the time. I like the woods okay, but not for more than a weekend at a time. I'll be a good-smelling city hippie.

In a yard up ahead, I spied a large snowdrift against an orange house. They must have been old people—there hadn't been new snow in a week, and there wasn't a single footprint in the yard. Snow at houses where the people have kids doesn't stay pure for long.

"Pardon me, Marianne," I said, as formally as I could manage. "I have to go."

And I ran as fast as I could, right into whoever's yard it was, and dove face-first into the drift. The snow got into the hood of my coat and onto my face, and even into my ears. It slipped past my gloves, got up my sleeves, and stung my bare wrists. It was awesome.

After I got home, it was time to put Operation: None of the Above into action.

First, I casually told my mother that I was thinking of not entering the spelling bee. It was important that I tell my mother—she's not quite as nutty as my father. Then again, most squirrels eat breakfasts that aren't as nutty as my father. There was no way I'd ever talk Dad into letting me out of any activities, but Mom might be persuaded. It wouldn't be easy, though.

"Not entering?" my mother asked, making just as nasty a face as I'd hoped she would. Mom makes some really super faces when she's upset. "Well, of course you're going to enter! And you're going to win! Your only real competition is from that snot-nosed little brat Marianne Cleaver. And we'll take her down by any means necessary!"

It's weird how much my parents hate Marianne, considering that she's probably the daughter they always wanted. Even I don't *hate* Marianne, exactly. It isn't her fault she's so dull—some people are just born that way. But if my dad could have used nuclear weapons to help me beat her at spelling, he probably would have done it.

"I don't know, Mom," I said. "I'm a bit worried that I've forgotten a lot of words lately."

"Don't worry about that," said Mom. "We'll make you some flash cards or something to do in the car. Now hurry up and get ready for flute practice. Mr. Porter says you haven't seemed very focused lately."

I had never been focused on my flute lessons. I usually spent the lessons wondering how far up Mr. Porter's nose I could stick my flute. I suspected that it was quite a long way. The guy has a schnoz the size of a Toyota.

"Mom," I asked, going in for the most important part of my plan, "don't you think I should maybe skip flute practice this week so I can study for the bee? Please? I need to work hard if I'm going to beat Marianne. She has a photographic memory, and she's going to use it to memorize the dictionary."

"Oh she is, is she?" Mom said. She paused and thought for a moment. "That's just like her. I'll tell you what, Jennifer. You can stay home from flute practice for the next two weeks, but that's all. And you'll be using that time to study."

"Okay!" I said. And I bounded up to my room. The plan was off to a perfect start!

So, free of the flute, at least, I grabbed my warmest blanket and curled up on my bed, leaning my back against the wall. My cat, Falstaff, came and sat next to me—he tried to sit on my lap, but since he's approximately the fattest cat in the universe, I didn't let him. Instead, he curled up beside me and rubbed his head against my thigh.

I grabbed my copy of *The Complete Works of Shakespeare* off my bookshelf and officially began my practice of None of the Above studying.

Of all the clubs I'm in, the only one I really like is the Shakespeare Club—partly because it's about the only one where Marianne isn't there. It's not a club sponsored by the school, the Y, or anything else, it's just a group of people who get together to talk about Shakespeare at a bookstore in Cornersville Trace. I'm the youngest person there by about twenty years, and I don't always know what they're talking about, but there's always someone there who can explain what's going on to me. We'd spent the last few meetings talking about *Titus Andronicus*, a play where a guy kills kids and feeds them to their parents. They never assign us any books like that in class! People would complain that they were "inappropriate."

But, anyway, I'm getting off track, aren't I? I'm supposed to be telling you about my dad, and what he had to do with what happened at the spelling bee. Don't worry. I'm getting to it.

That night, at dinner, my mother took a break from annoying me while Dad asked me to spell words like "myxomatosis" and "obdused."

"Did she tell you what that Marianne Cleaver girl is doing, Mitchell?" my mother asked him. "She's *memorizing* the *dictionary*." She rolled her eyes, as though she had just said Marianne was *roller-skating* to *Japan*.

"Oh she is, is she?" my father grumbled. "I'll just bet she is."

"She told Jennifer she has a photographic memory," Mom said.

"Yeah, right!" said Dad. "She's just covering up. I'll bet I know what's really going on here."

"What?" asked Mom.

"She's probably just memorizing the school's master word list, that's what."

"Cheating!" my mother exclaimed.

"She can't have the word list," I said. "They keep it locked up in a filing cabinet in the office."

"That's what they want you to think," said my father, in that horrible, patient voice people use to explain things to little kids. "Her dad probably bribed the secretary. She's probably at home memorizing that list now, and saying she's going to memorize the entire dictionary so no one suspects. Ha!"

"No!" I said. "She's really trying to memorize the dictionary."

"I doubt that very much," said Dad. "And I'll bet that brat Jason Keyes found a way to get ahead, too. And probably Harlan Sturr. Those kids are no good. But don't worry—we'll get you a copy of that list, too!"

"No, Dad!" I said. "You'd have to break into the school or something. It wouldn't be legal!"

"Jennifer," said my father, "if this were a perfect world, I'd agree with you. It's wrong. But Marianne and Jason probably both have the word list, and it's wrong for them to have it, too. When you grow up and start to get ahead in the corporate world, you'll learn that sometimes the only way to beat the cheaters is to do what they're doing, only better."

Now, don't get the wrong idea. My dad is not a criminal, normally. But there's something about the all-school bee that really gets into some people's heads around here. It does things to them. Crazy things.

I know you're supposed to have pride in your town, but I really, really don't like Preston. I can't wait till next year, when we'll all be at the middle school in Cornersville Trace. I think that if Preston had its own high school, this would be one of those towns where everything revolves around the high school football team. As it is, the all-school spelling bee at Gordon Liddy Community School is about as big an event as Preston ever has of its own. And some people in town—a lot of people—seem like they live for it.

And, though I always thought people took it too seriously, I never could have imagined that it could make them go quite as nuts as it did this year.

2
MUTUAL

pachyderm—noun. Any of various non-ruminant quadruped hoofed mammals having very thick skin: elephant; rhinoceros; hippopotamus. *When you call 911 to tell them a large pachyderm is charging into your house, they will ask you if you mean an elephant, a rhinoceros, or a hippopotamus.*

My parents did not wish for me to talk to you at first. But once I told them your goal was to get school officials in trouble, they changed their minds. They have believed for years that the officials were corrupt. That is why they never let me attend school until the bee began.

And I have a secret to tell you, to begin with. I knew all along that homeschooled children were allowed to enter the district bee. I had seen a page about it in the official rules of national spelling bees. But I tore the page out so my parents would not see it. They believed I had to be enrolled at the school to enter the bee. And I wanted to be enrolled. It was the most corrupt thing I had ever done. Please do not tell them about it.

I suppose you could say that before the spelling bee, and before I came to Gordon Liddy Community School, I was a very naive person. My parents did not let me out of the house very often. Even going to visit other homeschooled children was out of the question, because most of them were "no better than the public school kids." They were corrupt, immoral, and full of germs. So you can imagine that my parents were very nervous about letting me go to school in Preston, which they referred to as a "big city," even though it is actually a small town.

On my first day, the day I was to sign up for the spelling bee, they drove me to the school very early in the morning, and then made me sit in the car with them, staring up at the front door, for a very long time.

"Are you sure this is wise, Norman?" my mother asked my father. "Letting him in there?"

"He can take care of himself, Norma. We raised him right."

Mother turned back to look at me. "You be very careful in there, Mutual," she said. "I know what goes on in places like this, and we do not want you to be hurt. And do not let the other children give you a hard time. They will surely try. I know their tricks and manners."

"Yes, ma'am," I said.

"When you're in the classroom, you just sit quietly and don't talk to anybody," Mother continued. "There are bad kids in there. And they are all just going to be dying to turn you into a bad kid, too, Mutual. At recess, just sit on the steps and read from your dictionary. That playground equipment might look tempting, but it is dangerous!"

"Yes, ma'am," I said again. These were probably the two words I said most often in the days before I came to school: "yes" and "ma'am." Now they are probably "oh" and "crap." I had never even heard the word "crap" before I came to Gordon Liddy. As I said, I was very naive in the days before the spelling bee.

"Now, listen to the teacher, but do not listen too carefully. She will probably be just as bad as the kids are, and she will probably just be teaching the things we taught you when you were six. I do not care how you do on any tests, and I do not care what sort of grades you get. We know you are smart. Just sit there and think about spelling. And do not let anyone breathe on you, or you might catch a virus. Understand?"

"Yes, ma'am."

"Good. We can go inside now."

We stepped out of the car, and my father made sure that my tie was not crooked, and that I did not have any wrinkles in my blazer, which, of course, I did not.

My parents had never allowed me even to join an activity that might expose me to violence, corruption, or germs. Or other children, for that matter. We did not have a television set or a radio, except for a radio in the car that we never used. They spent a lot of time telling me that the "outside world" was a dangerous, immoral place. But when they found out that I was a good speller, they became determined that I should become a spelling bee champion. They had been talking to me about it since I was six.

My life had been mapped out ever since then—I was to become one of history's greatest spellers, joining the ranks of such famous spellers as Paul "Gerund" Malone and Janet "Diphthong" Kowalski. I was rather surprised to find that most people in the "outside world" had never heard of these people.

Because they believed that a student has to be registered in a school to participate in a spelling bee, and to qualify for the district bee, my parents decided to register me at Gordon Liddy Community School, at least until after the district bee was over.

Gordon Liddy Community School was a very long way from our house. My parents picked it because it had only one class per grade, which they say is more like things were in the "good old days." I am not sure when those days were, exactly. Sometimes I thought they meant the 1970s, other times I thought they meant biblical days.

When we opened the doors to the school, I expected that the inside of the school would be filthy, with drug dealers standing in the hall, and kids waiting around the corner, ready to jump out and beat me up for my milk money. Maybe there would be policemen pounding some ne'er-do-wells with billy clubs in the hall.

I was surprised to find that it was well lit and clean inside, and that all the kids I saw walking by outside the office looked just like ordinary, happy children, not like hooligans, and none of them seemed too ignorant to tie their own shoes. I thought I saw some graffiti, but it turned out to be a poster for the bee.

This was not what I had expected at all. Where were all the gang members?

Within five seconds of stepping into the school, I began

to wonder, just a little, about how honest my parents had been with me when they told me what the "outside world" was like. Or if they even knew what they were talking about.

Once inside the office, we waited silently in front of an empty desk until a woman came over to talk to us. She was a little wrinkly, and her hair was a bit of a mess, but she did not look scary or corrupt to me.

"Can I help you?" she asked.

"We are the Scriveners, Norm and Norma," said Mother. "This is our son, Mutual."

The woman smiled. "Well, hello, Mutual!" she said. "Welcome to Gordon Liddy. I'm Mrs. Rosemary, Principal Floren's secretary. You'll be in sixth grade, right?"

I was still too afraid to say anything at that point.

"He is eleven," said Mother.

"Yes." Mrs. Rosemary nodded. "Sixth grade. Now, you must be his father?"

She offered her hand to Father, who nodded, but did not shake it.

"That is Norman, his father," said Mother. She does most of the talking. "Now, before we leave our son in your care, we have a few requests."

"Of course."

"Mutual will also not be participating in physical education, science, or politics classes. We will continue his education in those fields at home."

"We don't really teach politics," said Mrs. Rosemary, "but we can arrange for him to go to the library during science and gym."

Mrs. Rosemary probably assumed that Mother was a

religious type who had something against science. In reality, however, Mother was afraid that they might talk about blood, guts, or poisonous spiders and snakes, and that I would get scared. She and my father are not really religious at all, unless believing in the "good old days" is a religion, and I do not think it is. I could be wrong, though.

Five minutes later, after some questions about the nutritional value of the school lunch, which I would not be eating anyway, and a few questions about the number of violent crimes which had occurred in the halls that year (none), my parents were back in the parking lot, probably sitting in the car, staring at the school as though they were expecting it to catch fire at any minute, and Mrs. Rosemary was escorting me to Mrs. Boffin's class. She seemed very friendly. Lots of children stared at me, but not one of them appeared to be mean, and most of them appeared to be fairly well groomed.

Having wondered all my life what school would be like, and having heard lectures about the "tricks and manners" of public school students day in and day out for weeks, I must admit that I was terribly disappointed.

3
CHRISSIE

Excerpt from notebook #43:
Tony Ostanek thinks people believe he's only scratching his nose when he picks it.

They say that everyone, everywhere, has secrets that make
them a mystery to everyone else. That isn't quite true,
though. They aren't always that much of a mystery. Most of
them are just waiting for someone who knows how to find
them out. Like I do.

Most kids in school have no idea just how much I know
about them. I know when they're going to act up, even before they do, probably. You school board types don't spend
much time in the hallways, but you'll have to take my word
for it that the halls were an awful lot safer when I was
the hall monitor. I was the best one the school ever had.
Everyone knows it.

By the end of second grade, I had filled nearly thirty
notebooks with information about the school and my
classmates—everything from "the peeled paint on the

radiator looks like a hot-air balloon" to things like "Gunther has his name written on his underwear in block letters."

I know that Jennifer Van Den Berg hates going to after-school clubs. I know Tony Ostanek's favorite video games. I even know what sort of stretching exercises Mrs. Rosemary does at her desk every morning. I know things that people probably think are total secrets. By fourth grade, I was more than a hall monitor. I was like the school's official detective. They even sent me interoffice memos now and then with assignments.

Which is how I found out exactly how bad things are messed up around here.

See, usually the office memos look something like this:

INTEROFFICE MEMO
FROM: Principal Floren
TO: Chrissie Woodward

Rumor has it that Harlan Sturr was seen purchasing spray paint at the hardware store. See if you can find out what he's up to.

But a few months ago, they sent me the wrong one.

It was just a couple of days after Harlan started the Rubber Band War to End All Rubber Band Wars. The school was starting to crack down on the combatants, and I had sent a detailed list of everyone involved—and where they had gotten their rubber bands—to the office.

That afternoon, I found a memo that they left on my desk by accident.

It said:

INTEROFFICE MEMO
FROM: Principal Floren
TO: Mrs. Boffin

Send Jake Wells to the office at once. He is not only the main supplier of weaponry to both armies of the rubber band war, he almost certainly has a rubber band in his lunch bag today— a flagrant violation of the new addition to our zero-tolerance weapons policy. Let's see those punks at the school board say I'm "soft on trouble-making" now!

Jake was in trouble. And it was all my fault.

All I had told them was that Jake Wells usually had a rubber band in his lunch to hold the plastic wrap over his broccoli crowns, and that some of them probably ended up getting fired in the war, so they could tell him not to bring them anymore. I never said he was the "main supplier"! In fact, he hadn't even been *involved* in the rubber band war! Floren was just punishing him to impress the school board!

I felt terrible about it. I'd gotten Jake in trouble over nothing. I kept the memo instead of passing it to Mrs. Boffin, but they just sent another one later. Jake had to miss recess for a week.

When I looked into the window during recess and saw Jake sitting at his desk, all alone, I started to realize that I'd been investigating the wrong side all these years.

After all, everyone knows that no matter how bad kids get, adults are the REAL criminals in the world, right? No offense, guys, but it's true. You don't see kids going around starting wars, do you? Well, rubber band wars, maybe, but not the kind with missiles. I'd been protecting the school from the students for years, but I should have been protecting the students from the school! I had believed that the school had our best interests in mind and that justice would prevail. Looking back, I can't believe how stupid I was.

How many other kids had I gotten in real trouble over something small that I'd reported just so I'd have something to report that day? Lots, probably.

The more I thought, the more I remembered. I sent a memo saying Marianne was reading a study guide during SSR, when we were supposed to be reading regular books, and they set up a time with her to meet with the librarian to find books she'd like. But when I sent a memo saying Tony was reading a video game magazine, he got detention.

Looking back over my notes, I saw this sort of thing happen over and over again, and I noticed a pattern. Kids who were good at spelling, like Marianne and Harlan, almost never got in trouble. Kids who weren't likely to have a shot at nationals, like Jake, got in trouble all the time.

I felt sick to my stomach. I don't think I'll ever be the same. Like in those cop movies where a guy's partner gets killed, and then he finds out that the sheriff let the killer get away because they're related. After that, he has to go out on his own. The previews for them usually start with some guy going, "In a world where he couldn't believe in anything . . . he believed in himself." Or sometimes it's "he believed in revenge," if it's a really violent one.

That's what the school was to me in the aftermath of Jake getting in trouble over the rubber band war. A world where I couldn't believe in anything. Except myself. And revenge.

I know that you people on the school board have no idea what REALLY goes on in here, so let me explain how the spelling bees work, exactly.

Every class has a class bee every year. They're really just for fun. And for grade grubbers like Marianne Cleaver to show off all of their spelling skills.

The bee that *matters* is the all-school bee on the first Friday in February—February 1 this year. To qualify for it, students have to pass a written test in January. Most sixth graders who take the written test can pass it, and about half of the fifth graders can. Only a handful of third and fourth graders ever qualify, and I've never seen a first or second grader make it.

At the all-school bee, the last five people left get to go on to the district bee in March, where they compete against kids from Shaker Heights and Cornersville Trace and other towns for the chance to move up to the nationals in Washington, D.C.

Now, the fact that you get to miss a day of school for the district bee is enough to get most kids to want to enter all by itself. But since the bee is such a big deal in town, they even put it on local TV. Even the kids who couldn't care less about spelling want to get on TV. Plus the bee is a huge deal here. Everyone has been looking forward to sixth grade— the year they're most likely to make it—all their lives. And some of them will stop at nothing to go to districts— cheating, sabotage, you name it. Bee season is my busy season as a hall monitor.

So, on the Tuesday morning when they'd be holding the written test, I started making notes right away, in a crisp new notebook, about everyone in the room. I'd be so busy investigating that I wasn't even entering myself. I had more important work to do.

"Good morning, class," said Mrs. Boffin. Every morning she says "Good morning" as though she expects the class to respond by saying "Good morning, Mrs. Boffin" in unison, but we never do. Only Marianne, teacher's pet extraordinaire, said "Good morning" back.

Even I don't know exactly how old Mrs. Boffin is. She's older than middle-aged, but still not exactly *old*. She says things like "lovely" and "delightful," never "cool" or "neat." You'd never guess that such a sweet old lady would work for such a corrupt school system.

"Now let's all take our seats," said Mrs. Boffin, even though everyone already had. "Before we start in on our usual activities, I'm sure you're all aware that today is the sign-up for the all-school spelling bee. The first-place winner this year will receive a new dictionary and a seventy-five-dollar gift certificate to Hedekker's Appliance Store."

Several people said "Oooh" sarcastically. You'd think that, since the bee was such a big deal, they'd come up with better prizes. Last year it was a gift certificate to a map store. But coming in first isn't really that big of a deal—the important thing for most people was getting to districts. If you go to districts, you get treated like a celebrity around town.

"Now, as you know, to qualify for the all-school bee, you'll have to pass the written test today after school. I'll now take the names of students who would like to sign up, and submit the list to the office. Who would like to sign up?"

"Wait, we have to sign up just to take the written test?" I asked. "Why can't we just show up for it?"

"Because these are the rules," said Mrs. Boffin.

I'm a firm believer in rules, of course. Or I was, anyway. But right about then, I was starting to figure out that you have to question everything that seems wrong. Why did they need a list of kids who wanted to take the written test? I know it doesn't seem like a big deal, but I made a note of it. I was going to be making notes of EVERYTHING the school did that was suspicious. We hadn't had to sign up like that last year.

Mrs. Boffin looked out across the room at all of the students holding up their hands. Practically everyone was signing up except for me. "We'll start at the back of the room," she said, setting the sign-up sheet on her desk. "Amber Hexam?"

Amber was crossing her arms over her chest, rocking back and forth, and chanting something under her breath. Amber considers herself to be pretty good at occult-type stuff, like casting spells, and I guessed she was trying to curse the other kids who were signing up for the bee. There are no rules against doing that, though, so I let it slide. And it's not like I've ever seen anything to make me think she could really get any spells to *work*, anyway.

She got up, made her way to the front of the room, wiggled her fingers in front of her face for a second, spun around three times, then wrote her name on the sheet.

"Jason Keyes?" Mrs. Boffin called.

Jason "Skeleton" Keyes was wearing a shirt with the logo for a heavy-metal band on it and trying to look tough, like he did every other day. As far back as kindergarten, I've heard him brag about vandalizing school property, breaking things on purpose, and doing all sorts of weird things to scare old ladies, though he never actually did any of it. He was all talk. Deep down, he wasn't that bad of a kid. In cop movies, cops would pick him out of the gang of bad kids and turn him around, I'll bet.

Jason shrugged his shoulders, stood up, and slowly lumbered toward Mrs. Boffin's desk, where he signed the sheet. During the walk back to his desk, he leaned over to me and said, "I'll give you ten bucks if you tell me how to break into the office and get the list." I scowled at him, and he walked past.

It was well known that the word list was kept somewhere in the office, but, contrary to popular belief, it isn't that hard to get into the office after hours, and it isn't that hard to find out which filing cabinet they keep the word list in. It isn't even that hard to find out the combination to unlock it. After all, I've known it since third grade.

"Jake Wells?"

Jake got up, and a couple of kids called out, "Go, Chow, go!"

Jake makes a pretty good living in the lunchroom as the Kid Who Will Eat Anything for a Dollar, which has earned him the nickname of Chow. He walked up to the front of the room, nervously put his name on the sheet, and sat back down. I wondered why he was bothering to enter—he never did very well in the "spelling practice" that we'd been having every day since winter vacation. He probably just wanted to get on TV.

"Tony Ostanek?"

Tony walked up without a word, signed up, and returned to his seat. He hated spelling. But I knew that his parents had promised him a new video game if he entered, and three of them if he won. I'd be watching him, too. He'd go to great lengths—even cheating, maybe—to get three new games.

"Jennifer Van Den Berg?"

Jennifer sat at her desk, keeping her hand in the air, but not standing up.

"Jennifer?" Mrs. Boffin repeated. "You're signing up, right?"

Jennifer sighed. "I guess so," she said, finally. And she walked up and signed the sheet.

"Marianne Cleaver?"

Marianne stood up and walked quickly to the front of the room to the sign-up sheet. She doesn't swing her arms when she walks, which makes her look like some sort of android. Maybe she actually is an android. It would explain a lot of the unanswered questions that I have about her.

As Mrs. Boffin slowly went through everyone else, I watched Jason as he leaned over toward Amber's desk. They talked in class a lot—from their spot in the back of the room, they could get away with talking quite a bit without Mrs. Boffin hearing them. But *I* could hear them. And I knew that they had huge secret crushes on each other.

"How'd you do in the class bee last year?" Jason asked Amber.

"Not well," she said. "But I didn't know all of the spells that I know now. Or as many curses."

Then they started passing notes. They did that when they didn't want kids around them—like me—to know what they were saying.

In the front of the room, Mrs. Boffin was finally calling Harlan Sturr's name.

When you show up to class and see a live goat wandering the hallways, or find a couple of the doors to classrooms duct-taped shut, you can bet Harlan was involved. Most of his pranks are very small-time, like stealing chalk, or doing impressions of the teachers when they aren't looking. Your basic class clown business. But every year Harlan has to sit at the desk closest to the teacher's to keep him out of trouble. He didn't even get up to sign up for the bee; he just leaned over to Mrs. Boffin's desk and put his name down.

Just as Mrs. Boffin was about to fold up the sign-up sheet and ask someone to deliver it to the office, there was a knock at the door. "Come in," she called.

In the doorway stood Mrs. Rosemary and a kid in a blazer and tie. He had a bowl cut—the kind you normally see on five-year-olds.

"Oh!" said Mrs. Boffin. "The new student! Please, come inside!"

A new kid!

He and Mrs. Rosemary stepped into the room, and every eye focused on the new kid. He was, hands down, the weirdest-looking kid I'd ever seen in person. Besides the blazer and the bowl cut, his face looked as though a five-hundred-pound safe had fallen on it, flattening all of his features, except for his lips, which stuck out from the rest of his face as though they were held out by invisible clothespins.

"Good morning," said Mrs. Rosemary. "Everyone, this is Mutual Scrivener. He'll be joining your class."

"Welcome, Mutual," said Mrs. Boffin. "What a wonderfully interesting name you have!"

Mutual said nothing.

"Well, Anita," said Mrs. Boffin to Mrs. Rosemary, "since you're here, I have the list of students who would like to take the written test ready. I was just about to give it to one of the students."

"Is that the list?" Mutual said, opening his mouth for the first time since setting foot in the room.

"Why, yes it is," said Mrs. Boffin. "I didn't imagine you'd want to jump right into entering on your first day!"

"I'd like to, please," he said. I noticed his face scrunching up as Mrs. Boffin breathed on him with her coffee breath. Mrs. Boffin's coffee breath can knock a kid out—everyone else knew to stand back when she was talking to them. She handed Mutual the list and the pen, and I watched as he carefully added his name to the last spot on the list.

"Lovely!" said Mrs. Boffin. "Now, Mutual, would you like to tell the class a little bit about yourself?"

"I would prefer not to, please," said Mutual, quietly.

"What a goober!" Tony said under his breath.

"Wow," I heard Jason mutter to Amber. "That kid may look like a geek, but he sure has guts to talk to a teacher like that!"

Mrs. Boffin paused. "Well, that's all right, too. It's

33

perfectly normal to be shy, especially on the first day. Why don't you take your seat? You'll be over there, next to Jason."

Mutual slowly moved over to the empty desk in the back of the room, and Jason did his best to look threatening. He made sure his T-shirt, which had the logo of the band Paranormal Execution above a picture of demons riding motorcycles, was clearly visible, and Mutual stared at it as though he'd never seen a demon on a motorcycle before.

As he walked, I noticed that, in addition to a belt, he was wearing suspenders under his blazer. This meant that of all the kids in school, or maybe the state, he was probably the least likely to have his pants fall down. I wrote that down in capital letters. It was going to make it pretty hard to figure out what kind of underwear he wore, but I was going to have to find out. I knew that sort of thing about everyone else, of course, and there was no way I was going to let that kind of data go unrecorded on a kid this weird.

A minute after he took his seat, Mrs. Boffin was talking about Christopher Columbus, and Mutual was staring at his desk, not taking notes or anything. I tried to look like I was taking notes about Columbus myself, but I was actually writing down everything I could about Mutual. Luckily for me, Amber and Jason did their best to get him talking.

"Hey, kid," Amber whispered at him. "Aren't you going to take notes?"

Mutual shook his head, and Amber chuckled.

"Well," said Jason, "you'll fit in pretty well back here. We don't pay attention, either! You can talk if you want to. Boffin won't be able to hear you if you aren't too loud."

"Yeah," said Amber. "She's so old she can't hear anything past the first couple of rows."

"Are you trying to corrupt me?" asked Mutual, still whispering.

Jason and Amber laughed. "Corrupt you?" asked Jason, through giggles. "On your first day?"

Mutual said nothing.

"Why?" asked Jason. "Aren't you corrupt already?"

Mutual shrugged. I wondered what Mrs. Boffin was thinking, putting him right next to Jason. The kid was obviously an easy target.

"Come on," said Jason, who, I could tell, was trying to think of the best ways to freak the new kid out. "Haven't you ever stolen all the chalk from a classroom?"

Mutual shook his head. Jason hadn't, either, really. Only Harlan *really* did that sort of thing. But I could tell from the shocked look on his face that Mutual believed that Jason had.

"Really?" Amber whispered. "You mean you never stole anyone's underwear and ran it up the flagpole?"

Again, Mutual shook his head. Neither Jason nor Amber had ever actually done this, either, but, again, Mutual obviously believed they had. Jason tried to push it a step further.

"Haven't you ever even danced naked in a school cafeteria?" he asked.

Mutual's eyes got so wide that it was a miracle they didn't fall into his lap. Again, he shook his head. Surely he didn't believe that anyone had done that! Who was this kid? Had he just been living under a rock all his life?

"Really?" Amber laughed. "Everyone's done that! It's part of growing up."

"Well," said Jason, giggling, "if you need to be corrupted, we'll see to it. But you've got a long, long way to go."

For the first time since he'd been in the class, Mutual smiled a little.

4

Jason—
Writing this down so Mutual can't hear you. What do you think of him?
—Amber

A—
I dunno. Poor kid. His parents make him get all dressed up just to go to school!

Seems like he doesn't get out much. Five bucks says he's never heard a metal song in his life.
—J

Yeah, probably not. Looks like we've got our work cut out for us. I'll cast a spell for luck.
—A

Go for it! Ah, nothing like a fresh young mind to corrupt. I should be a teacher!
—J

You, a teacher? Hahahahahahaha.
—A

You think he's just here so he can be in the bee?
—J

Probably. I'll bet he's homeschooled or something.
—A

They have to let homeschooled kids compete in the
bee if they want to. It's in the rule book. I'll ask
him if he knows that later on.
—J

5

HARLAN

defenestrate—verb. To throw someone or something out of a window. *On particularly dull days, Jason and Amber would tell people that they were plotting to defenestrate the teacher.*

Okay, Chrissie. I have one secret that I'll bet you don't know about. Unless you've been inside my bedroom, digging through my stuff.

Here it goes:

I spend a lot of time planning my own funeral. I have five whole pages' worth of plans for it.

Now, don't get the wrong idea. I'm perfectly healthy and all that. Heck, if I don't get hit by a car or something, I'll probably live to a ripe old age. My great-grandpa is ninety, you know. And by the time I get that old, they'll probably have a cure for old age, right?

But it still scares the heck out of me to think that I'll have to die sooner or later. I've never told this to anyone—class clowns aren't supposed to think of morbid stuff like that. But once you're dead, that's it. You've played your last joke. Your last chance to be remembered is gone. Unless you have a really awesome funeral, like I'm going to.

My funeral is going to have jugglers and clowns and a laser light show. And I'm going to have a tombstone with my face carved on it, and when people walk by, it'll spit water out at them. That way I'll be able to keep playing jokes on people for years after I'm dead, and when people get spit at, they'll go, "Who was this Harlan Sturr guy?" and go try to find out about me. Whenever I start thinking about death, it always cheers me up to think about my funeral and my tombstone (which, by the way, will say, "Here lies Harlan Sturr. Please don't pee on him").

Also, I may or may not be buried in the middle of a busy street. I haven't decided yet. I think it would be kind of cool to be right under a traffic light—don't ask me why, but I do. And I want to see if my service in the Rubber Band War to End All Rubber Band Wars, the Great November Food Fight, and the Three-Bean Casserole War can get me a spot in the veterans' cemetery first.

I was scared about finishing sixth grade for a lot of the same reasons. I'd pulled some good pranks in my day, but I didn't think I'd pulled any pranks that people were really going to remember. I mean, the goat thing was great, but they remembered the goat, not me.

That was what I was thinking when I taped all the doors shut that one time—I thought it was the sort of thing people would remember. But they didn't. They'd gotten them opened by the time most people got to school. And I couldn't take credit for it without getting in trouble. (I'm only saying it was me NOW because you promised I wouldn't get in trouble for it—and I'd better not!)

So none of my pranks had made me a legend. Not the goat. Not the doors. Not the Rubber Band War to End All Rubber Band Wars. I still hadn't really left my mark.

Not like Johnny Dean.

I'm sure you know about him. Johnny Dean was in sixth grade back when we were in preschool—I guess he's in college by now. But in sixth grade, when Principal Floren brought his dog to school, Johnny somehow managed to paint the dog purple, and brought it out onstage right in the middle of the assembly where everyone was watching the Good Times Gang, those singers that Floren likes so much. Even now, every kindergartner still hears about Johnny Dean. The guy's a legend.

And it used to depress me to think that soon I'd leave Gordon Liddy behind and most people a grade or two below me would forget that I was ever here. But then I came up with a plan for the all-school spelling bee. If I could pull it off, I'd go down in school history for sure. All I had to do was get to the top five in the bee.

After school on Tuesday, the written test only took about five minutes. It was a pretty easy—everyone in class who took it passed. But, anyway, you wanted me to talk about the stuff I thought was unusual at the written test, right?

Well, for one thing, most of the words on it were words we've had in regular spelling tests already this year. It's almost like they wanted to make sure that all of the sixth graders would qualify. All of them did, after all. Even Jake. And I thought it was kind of weird that they even needed a list of who was taking it to start with. They didn't do that last year.

Plus, Principal Floren was walking around the room the whole time while we took the test, taking a lot of notes and muttering under his breath and sweating a lot. Everyone knows that Floren is one sweaty guy, but it's always weird to see someone sweating in January.

Then, after school, my mom decided we should celebrate the fact that I qualified for the bee by going down to Burger Baron, and Principal Floren was there. He was sitting in a corner booth with a couple of old bums—I think one of them was that guy Mr. Agnew, who used to be the janitor before they fired him a few years ago. And he looked terrible, like he hadn't had a bath since he got fired. He, Floren, and some other guy were all talking really quietly, and when he saw me, Floren kind of turned up his collar and tried to keep me from seeing that it was him. But I did.

Have you ever been to Burger Baron? Everyone in town knows about it, since it's been there forever, but few people ever go inside. I had never been before, myself. The food was pretty lousy, and it smelled like a butt that someone tried to cover with perfume, only you could still smell the butt underneath the flowery smell. Floren and that band of scuzzy-looking guys were the only other people there.

They certainly seemed like they were up to something, but I didn't think much more about it at the time. I don't normally go around looking for clues, you know.

That's your job, Chrissie.

6
MUTUAL

corrupt—adjective. Immoral and dishonest, using one's position for personal gain illegally. *Jason figured that if he was ever arrested for frightening an old lady, he could pay a corrupt judge to declare him innocent.*

I was quiet during the ride home after my first day at Gordon Liddy. School was not nearly as scary as my parents had always made it out to be. Lots of kids tried to talk to me, and only a couple of them really seemed at all strange. None of the students seemed like hooligans, except for Jason and Amber, but even they seemed friendly, in their own way. Perhaps they were trying to trick me into becoming a bad kid, but they were being very nice about it.

I had overheard Jason talking about Paranormal Execution—the words on top of his shirt. At first I did not think those words made any sense, but I came to realize that it was a musical group of some sort. I wondered what they sounded like, and hoped that I could find out soon. It was safe to assume that they did not sing campfire songs, which were the only kind of songs I knew.

"Well, Mutual," Mother asked, "did you keep your mouth shut?"

"Yes, ma'am," I said.

"And did you pay attention to the teacher?"

"No, ma'am."

"Good boy. She was probably trying to indoctrinate you. Do that word."

"Indoctrinate," I said. "Verb. To teach doctrine as absolute truth until the indoctrinatee accepts it as fact. As in 'Television producers try to indoctrinate viewers into immoral philosophies.' I-N-D-O-C-T-R-I-N-A-T-E. Indoctrinate."

"Good boy."

My parents have been making me "do" words since I was six. To do a word means to pronounce it, define it, use it in a sentence, spell it, and then pronounce it again. In those days, it was my favorite game.

As we pulled out of the town and into the farmland that surrounded it, I looked out my window at the cows. I had, in fact, listened to the teacher, and very carefully, all day long, when Amber and Jason were not talking to me. I had waited patiently for Mrs. Boffin to start in with the indoctrination and the immoral values, but she had not done it. She had just talked about explorers all morning, then talked about math all afternoon. Maybe she had done the indoctrinating during the science class, when I had been excused to go to the library. Even there, I honestly expected to find nothing on the shelves but pornographic magazines and socialist pamphlets. But there had not been any.

Once again, I was terribly disappointed.

And recess was even stranger—while I sat on the steps outside the school, I pretended to read from my dictionary, but I was actually watching everybody. I expected that the children were going to divide into opposing gangs and have a rumble, but there was not even a scuffle. The younger children just played on swings and metal sliding boards. The older ones, including the students from my class, stood around talking or, in some cases, throwing balls back and forth. Nobody got hurt, as far as I could tell.

"Was the written test for the bee difficult?" Mother asked.

"Not at all," I said.

The written test was very boring. We had to sit on the floor of the gym with a pencil and a sheet of paper while Mrs. Rosemary read out fifteen very easy words. Principal Floren wandered around making notes the entire time. He seemed like a very strange man. He was the only person I saw who looked just as scary as my mother said he would be.

"Now," said Mother, as we turned into the wooded area that would, eventually, lead to our house, "did you find out who the best spellers were?"

"There was one girl named Marianne that I thought would be good."

"Why is that?"

"She answered every question the teacher asked, and she was always right."

"Ah," said Mother. "I bet they are using her to cheat, then. That is what they do—they pick their favorite students, and they brainwash them. Then, when the government comes to inspect the school, they just show them the students they have brainwashed. Right, Norman?"

"That is what they do," said Father, nodding.

"Right," said Mother. "They had her brainwashed into knowing all the answers, but they might not be able to help her during the spelling bee. They will surely try to cheat, though. We will have to be on the lookout for cheaters."

"Always vigilant." Father nodded.

"Do that one," Mother commanded me.

"Vigilant," I said. "Adjective. Carefully observant and on the lookout for danger. As in 'The boy was always vigilant against brainwashing and indoctrination.' V-I-G-I-L-A-N-T. Vigilant."

"Good. Who else looked like a good speller?"

I thought for a moment. "Jennifer Van Den Berg. She seemed smart."

"None of those children will really be smart, Mutual. They have been in that awful school all their lives."

This time I knew they were wrong. Jennifer was clearly very smart, and didn't seem awful or corrupt to me at all. She did not seem to pay much attention to the teacher, really, but when she was drawing in her notebook, or just sitting at the desk, reading, she would sort of talk to herself, and, when she did, she smiled a lot. It was as though she was living a whole different life in her head than the one she was living at school. I stared at that smile every chance I got.

"During sustained silent reading, she was reading a Shakespeare play," I said. She smiled the most during sustained silent reading. I had read from my dictionary, and had noticed Marianne and a few others were reading from larger ones than mine. I wished I had a Shakespeare book, too.

"Shakespeare?" asked Mother. "She probably has a dirty, perverted mind, then. Shakespeare's plays were just filthy. Right, Norman?"

"Filthy," Father agreed. "And violent."

I was not certain that they were correct in this. I had never read any Shakespeare before—I barely knew who he was. So I read about him when I went to the library during science and gym. I had read most of *Henry V,* one of his plays, during science, but Jennifer sort of ignored me when I asked her about it. I thought that perhaps it was the only one of his plays most people had read, and experts like her got tired of talking about it.

Father began to pull the car up to our little house, which was over a mile from the main road, and far enough from the town itself that no one would deliver a pizza to us. If you can believe it, I had never had a pizza before in my life. Today the thought of going a month without a pizza is enough to make me say "Oh, crap!" right out loud.

"Did anyone try to sabotage you as a speller?" asked Mother.

"No," I said.

"How about corrupt you?"

I thought about Jason and Amber's promise that they would corrupt me if I wished. I wondered if dancing naked in the cafeteria was really a part of growing up. None of the kids in the class seemed like the kind of person who would dance naked, and when they went to lunch, I certainly had not seen anyone doing it, though I kept looking around for someone doing such a thing. But no one had even danced in his underwear!

I sat still, staring straight ahead, for a minute after the car had been parked in front of the house, not saying anything. My parents stared back at me.

"No," I said, finally. "No one tried to corrupt me today."

"They must be waiting until you get comfortable, then," said Mother. "But they will. Just you wait! I know their tricks and their manners!"

Jason had promised to try to corrupt me. He had not done so yet, but he had given me the idea to become a "spelling hustler," which is a kind of person who goes into bars and makes money by getting people to bet him twenty dollars that he can spell any given word. He said that this was the best way to make money in spelling, and promised to teach me the tricks of the trade.

Corrupt or not, there was a lot that I could learn in a town like Preston. Things I could never learn on my own.

That night, before dinner, I sat in my room with a pen and a sheet of paper. I was supposed to be studying spelling words, but I was actually trying my hardest to draw the logo for Paranormal Execution.

7

JENNIFER

umpteen — adjective. Very many; used to express a number that is unspeakably high, although not as unimaginably high as a jillion or bazillion. *After Marianne got on my nerves umpteen times in one afternoon, I started to fantasize about defenestrating her.*

Tuesday afternoon, after the written test, I was stuck in the Spirit Squad room, making a bunch of stupid posters. That's really all we ever do in Spirit Squad—make posters. Spirit Squad is supposed to be like cheerleading, only there aren't really any teams to cheer for in town. So we make collages and posters for all the school events—or, if there isn't an event going on, we'll make posters about things like diversity, while Mrs. Jonson, the faculty sponsor, sits in the corner grading papers and sipping coffee. I was drawing a large bumblebee with markers and writing "BEE there or BEE square." And I was really, really bored.

"Isn't this a little trite?" I asked.

"Trite?" said Marianne. "As in boring or clichéd?"

"Yeah. I mean, a bumblebee on a spelling bee poster? Isn't it the same thing they do every year?"

Brittany Tatomir glanced up from the poster she was drawing, which said "Who will the winner BEE?," and looked at me. "Yeah," she said. "It's a bit lame, but what do you want to put on them instead? A grasshopper?"

"I don't know," I said. "Something different. Maybe a great speller from history."

"Like who?" asked Marianne. "Name any three people who are famous for their spelling skills."

"Noah Webster," I said, after thinking about it for a second. "The guy who wrote Webster's dictionary."

"Who the heck would recognize him if we put him on a poster?" asked Marianne. "I wouldn't, and if I don't, nobody else will, either."

I didn't fight her on this. Mostly because I wouldn't recognize Noah Webster myself unless he showed up on my porch holding a sign that said "Hi, I'm Noah Webster." And even then, I'd think it was probably just some nut in a costume, not Noah Webster. I hate it when Marianne makes good points.

"Fine," I said. "How about Shakespeare? People know what he looked like, don't they?"

Brittany looked up from her poster again. "Was he a good speller?" she asked. "I heard most writers stink at spelling."

"Actually," interrupted Mrs. Jonson, "nobody was a good speller back then. They didn't really have any rules of spelling in Shakespeare's day. They just spelled things however they thought they should be spelled, and figured people would know what they meant."

"Really?" I asked.

Mrs. Jonson barely looked up from grading papers, but she nodded.

"Wow," said Marianne. "If people just spelled things however they wanted, it must have taken weeks for anyone to lose a spelling bee!"

"Yeah," said Brittany. "It would have been a much harder sport in those days, huh?"

"Anyway," said Marianne, "that means we shouldn't put him on a spelling bee poster. As P-R-E-S-I-D-E-N-T of the Spirit Squad, I say we keep going with the bumblebee theme."

It's not like it mattered what was on the posters, anyway. The real reason to make posters for the spelling bee was just that they needed something for the Spirit Squad to do. The bee was going to be held during the day, so everyone in school would have to attend whether they liked it or not. And it was the talk of the town, anyway. There was no real reason to advertise it.

Twenty minutes later, Marianne looked up from her umpteenth bumblebee poster. "Hey," she said. "What did you guys think of that new kid?"

"Well," I said, "he sure seemed different."

I was pretty certain there had never been a kid at Gordon Liddy like Mutual Scrivener, the new kid. I'd never heard of a kid actually wearing a blazer and a tie to school when it wasn't picture day. No one quite knew what to make of him.

"I hear he moved in from a bigger town," said Brittany, "because his parents thought he had a better chance in the spelling bee here."

"Yeah," said Claire, a fifth grader. "I heard they home-schooled him and taught him nothing but spelling since he was, like, four. He already has the whole Webster's dictionary memorized, and now he's working on the American Heritage one."

"That's not true!" said Marianne, who was probably scared to death to see another kid studying the dictionary as carefully as she was. "If you ask me, he's either A, a freak, B, a mutant, or C, a jerk."

"What makes you say that?" I asked. "He didn't seem like a jerk. I thought he seemed nice."

"Nice? He was a total snob!" said Marianne. "He hardly said a word to anybody!"

"Maybe he was just nervous," I said. "Wouldn't you be?"

"You can just tell by looking at him that he's a jerk, can't you?" said Marianne. "And anyway, how smart can he be if he hasn't been in school a day in his life?"

"He looked pretty smart to me," said Claire.

"Ha!" said Marianne. "That's prejudice. Just because he had glasses doesn't make him smart," she said. "Look at me. I don't wear glasses, and I'm still smart."

"You saw him in spelling practice!" said Brittany. "He was fierce!"

We had a full hour of spelling practice in the afternoon, and it was very clear that Mutual knew his stuff. He hadn't missed a word. He hadn't even looked as though he had to think about any of them. He might have actually HAD the dictionary memorized.

"I'll bet he kicks your butt at the bee," I said, just to egg her on, though I sincerely hoped he would.

"Jennifer," Mrs. Jonson interrupted, "watch what you say. This is the Spirit Squad, girls, not the gossip club. Let's not spend our time saying mean things about your fellow students."

Actually, it WAS the gossip club. Almost all of the after-school clubs were really gossip clubs.

"Anyway," said Marianne, "he can't possibly study the dictionary as hard as I do. I did A and B last night, and tonight I'll do C and D."

"You did not!" I said, laughing.

"Did so!" she said. "Listen! Abnegation. A-B-N-E-G-A-T-I-O-N. Brecciated. B-R-E-C-C-I-A-T-E-D."

I have to admit that I was a bit impressed—Marianne *must* have been studying to even come up with words like those.

"Yeah," I said, "but what do those words even mean?"

"Who cares?" said Marianne. "You don't have to know what they mean, just how to spell them. Wasting your time with the definitions is a real rookie mistake for spelling bees, if you ask me. I'll bet the new kid reads the definitions."

"Well," I said, "what good is knowing how to spell a word if you don't even know what it means?"

"Duh!" said Marianne. "You can use it to win a spelling bee! And I have to cut corners wherever I can to get through the whole dictionary. Plus, everyone knows the new kid is probably cheating."

"What?" I asked.

"Yeah," said Claire. "I heard they're going to feed him the answers through some kind of high-tech earpiece. And Jason Keyes is going to steal the master word list. And I heard that Harlan is planning to slash the tires of the bus on the day of the bee so people can't get here!"

"That's nonsense," I said. "Harlan wouldn't do that."

Marianne snorted. "You've got a lot to learn about how spelling bees work, Jen," she said.

By the time Spirit Squad ended, it was nearly five o'clock. I ran as fast as I could to my mother's car, which was waiting right outside the school. I never got to walk home from Spirit Squad this time of year, since it would be getting close to dark out when it ended.

"I assume you passed the written test?" Mom asked.

"Yeah," I said.

"I knew you would," she said. "Who else took it?"

"Almost everybody," I said. "It was all words we had in spelling last year. Harlan and Amber both passed, too. And Brittany Tatomir, and Tony Ostanek, and Jake . . . and a new kid, too!"

"New kid?" my mother asked. "You have a new kid? Is he a good speller?"

"Yeah. Rumor has it that he's some kind of prodigy."

"Sounds like he'll be a tough contender, then. Drat. I was hoping it would just be between you and Marianne. What's his name?"

"Mutual," I said. "Mutual Scrivener."

"Mutual?" my mother said. "I'll bet his parents must be dirty hippies to name him something like that—they're always naming their kids things like Starflower, Love, or Togetherness."

She wrinkled her nose, like she was saying they named their kids Dirt, Garbage, or Idiot. I thought Starflower sounded like a nice name, actually. Maybe I'll change my name to Starflower when I become a hippie myself.

"Did this kid smell bad?" Mom asked. "Hippies always smell bad."

I wanted to say "Not ALL of them," but I didn't. I guess I hadn't really met any in real life, and you can't tell how someone smells based on TV.

"I don't think so," I said. "He was wearing a tie and a blazer."

"Well, they aren't hippies, then," said Mom. "You won't catch them wearing a tie. Was he foreign?"

"Didn't look like it."

"Well, then, I guess his parents are just weirdos. You should be able to beat him without too much trouble, right?"

"I suppose so," I said, though I really had no idea. We drove along in silence for a bit. "Hey, Mom," I said. "Did you know they didn't even have spelling rules when Shakespeare was alive?"

"Who told you that?" my mother asked.

"Mrs. Jonson, the faculty sponsor."

"That sounds like a myth to me, Jennifer. How could anyone even learn to read if they didn't have spelling in the first place?"

"She said people just spelled things however they thought they should be spelled, and people knew what they meant. She says Shakespeare even spelled his name in different ways."

"Hmmm," said my mother. "Do you think she's just trying to psych you out?"

"What would she do that for?" I asked.

"Well, maybe she's the person Marianne bribed for the word list, and she paid extra to have her sabotage other people. She's trying to get it into your head that people can spell things however they want, so you'll stop caring about spelling rules. Oh, that's sneaky of her!"

"I don't think she's being sneaky, Mom," I said. "Why would she do a thing like that?"

"Jennifer," my mother said with a sigh, "you've got a lot to learn about how the world works. There are good people out there, of course, but the corruption goes all the way up to the top, probably even at Gordon Liddy. It wouldn't be the first time in history that a teacher was trying to sabotage other students. Maybe the Cleavers are paying her. Or maybe Mutual's parents are in on it somehow."

"Or maybe it's the truth," I said. "Maybe they really didn't spell things in certain ways back then."

"Well, you can ask people at the next Shakespeare Club meeting, then," said my mother.

I was pretty sure she was just being crazy. I mean, surely no one was crazy enough to go around bribing Mrs. Jonson, right? I wished it was Shakespeare Club night, so I could find out for sure. But I wasn't sure WHERE the heck I was going that night. I had lost track.

"What activities do I have today?" I asked.

"You have indoor soccer at seven," said Mom.

"Can I skip it tonight so I can work on spelling?" I asked.

"I don't know, Jennifer."

"Please?" I asked. "Why do you keep making me play sports that I don't even like?"

"Parenting today is like developing a product," she said. "We're not just raising you, we're getting you ready to be marketed to colleges. It's what we did with Val. She signed up for everything, and that helped her get into a great school!"

Apparently it didn't occur to Mom that it might hurt my feelings to be treated like I was a new kind of cola. But it did. It always had. What was going to happen if I didn't win the bee? Would they change my formula? Get me a new look? Discontinue me?

They'd probably discontinue me, in a way. They'd send me off to military school, have another kid, and hope it'd be a better speller. I didn't think Mom would ever let Dad sign me up for military school over missing the recycling club or indoor soccer, but the bee was another matter. If I didn't even make it to districts in sixth grade, the year Val went all the way to nationals, they might decide it was time for drastic measures.

"But the spelling bee is the most important one right now, right?" I asked.

"I suppose so," said Mom.

"And I want to study for it as much as I can," I said. "The colleges won't know that I missed two weeks of indoor soccer. It can still be on my application, even if I just quit!"

Mom didn't say anything for a second. "All right," she said. "As long as you study spelling. I guess you can miss soccer if it gives you a better chance to win the bee."

"And if I go to districts, can I drop a few more of them?"

She thought about it. "I think that would probably be a good idea," she said. "I'll talk to your father."

I looked out my window, so she couldn't see that I was breathing a sigh of relief.

I felt like I had a pretty good chance of winning. Or at least making it to districts, which was all that really mattered. I guessed that Marianne, Mutual, and I would probably all make it—but I hoped that either Mutual or I was the winner. Anybody but Marianne. I wouldn't mind losing to Mutual as much.

In fact, I was kind of fascinated by Mutual. I'm not saying that I had a crush on him or anything, but I'd known every other guy in town since they were about four years old. The very fact that Mutual wasn't from Preston, as far as anyone knew, made him seem sort of . . . exotic. In a really weird way.

Plus, no one else knew this, but he talked to me on the way to recess. A little, anyway.

On the way to recess, he had asked me what I thought of *Henry V*, a play I'd never read. I was so embarrassed not to have read it that I hadn't said anything, I'd just sort of run away. He was probably an expert on Shakespeare. But I was going to read *Henry V* right away, so I could talk about it with him.

Finally. Someone I might really be able to talk to in Preston! I don't want to say I had a crush on Mutual, exactly, but I imagined us going head to head at the end of the spelling bee, and he'd be all impressed with how smart I was, and want to hang out with me every day after that.

I mean, I like to think I'm friends with everyone in class. We've all gotten to know each other really well over the years. But the truth is, there was no one like me in town.

Brittany is a lot smarter than she acts, but she's afraid that if anyone sees her jump in a snowdrift, they'll think she's weird. And Marianne's not exactly stupid either, but, well, she's nuts. I mean, I don't want to sound like a snob or anything, but sometimes I wished that there was someone in my class that I could go to Shakespeare Club meetings with. Someone else who was into that sort of thing. I wasn't sure Mutual had ever jumped in the snow, but maybe he'd try.

I mean, you know what I really hate? When we have to find a partner to work on something in class. Everyone else pairs up, and I start to panic, wondering who will want to work with me. I always wish I could just keep working by myself. But maybe Mutual would be someone I could always pick as a partner in class.

Plus, I hate to say my mom was right, but his parents probably WERE weirdos. In fact, they were probably just as nuts as mine. Maybe HE wanted to run away and be a hippie, too.

And, to top it all off, he was a guy.

No one's going to see this besides the school board people, right?

Good. Because I don't believe in violence, but if this gets out . . . well, let's just say that people who read Shakespeare learn an awful lot of interesting ways to murder people, Chrissie.

That evening I was back on my bed, stroking Falstaff behind the ears as he sat next to me—there certainly wasn't room on my lap for him, since *The Complete Works of Shakespeare* took up the whole thing. On the other side of me, the side where Falstaff wasn't, I had a dictionary. Every time I came upon a word in Shakespeare that I didn't know, which I did pretty regularly, I would look it up. For once, I actually felt like I was learning stuff, not just memorizing things long enough to get a grade off them. The None of the Above studying method was working!

At seven, my dad called me downstairs. I assumed it was dinnertime, but when I got downstairs, the table was empty.

"Look, Jennifer," he said. "Good news. I went to city hall today and got the blueprints."

"The blueprints?" I said. "What blueprints?"

"The ones for the school, silly," he said. "We'll need to study them really carefully. This is your ticket to getting a great job when you grow up!"

I suppose it's worth noting that my dad does not have a good job, exactly. He works for a big company, but his job is really to follow the boss around and agree with whatever he says. He likes to act like he's really important, but I know that his real job is being a PBK—professional butt kisser.

He laid out a large blue sheet of paper on the table, which was like a view of the inside of the school from above. It showed every room, hall, window, door, and bathroom.

"What's the point of this?" I asked. "I know my way around the school."

"Don't be so confident, honey," said my dad. "We can't leave anything to chance. Now, here's the office." He pointed down at the room near the front door, which I knew perfectly well was the office. "Do you know where they keep the word list?"

"In one of the file cabinets, I think," I said. "They're

along this wall, here. But two of them are locked, so you won't be able to get into them anyway." I pointed to the wall on the blueprint.

So there you have it. It's true. I told my dad where they keep the master list, which I guess makes me an accessory to the break-in.

"I see. Well, how are they locked? Is it just a cheap padlock?"

This was when I realized what Dad had in mind. I had hoped he was just going to have me do some weird exercise where I concentrate really hard on thinking about the filing cabinet. It wouldn't be the strangest thing he's tried. One time some wacko told him that if you listen to Mozart and stand on your head while you study, it helps you learn stuff. He tried to make me study while standing on my head for a good week. That was nuts. But this was the first time he had turned to crime.

"Dad, please," I said. "You don't need to break into the school!"

"You should be grateful, dear," said my mother, as she began to set the table for dinner. "Not every daddy would do that sort of thing for his daughter."

But I wasn't grateful. I was horrified.

I ran back up to my bedroom, got my Shakespeare book out, and tried as hard as I could to just focus on that instead of thinking about Dad. I even opened the window to make the room really, really cold, so the blankets would feel even better. I knew how much it bugged them when I opened the window when the heat was on; they usually came in shouting that we weren't trying to heat the whole stinking street. I guess it made me feel a bit better to do something that I knew annoyed them, even though I chickened out and closed it again after about five minutes.

I fell asleep with my light still on, Falstaff at my side, and the book open to *Macbeth*.

8

INTEROFFICE MEMO
FROM: Mrs. Boffin
TO: Mrs. Rosemary
Out of curiosity, why isn't Mutual taking science?
Yesterday he went to the library during science
and gym, and today his mother sent a note saying that if I don't "watch out," he may end up
there for history as well. Are his parents very
religious?

INTEROFFICE MEMO
FROM: Mrs. Rosemary
TO: Mrs. Boffin
I don't think so—they're just afraid of germs and
blood and guts.

INTEROFFICE MEMO
FROM: Mrs. Rosemary
TO: Principal Floren
Just had a call from Mrs. Scrivener—she'd like
to know if you're a member of the Brickcutters.
You know—those guys who drive the little cars
around in the parade. She thinks they're "in

charge of the whole world" and said to tell you that she knows your "tricks and manners."

INTEROFFICE MEMO
FROM: Principal Floren
TO: Mrs. Rosemary
Please tell them that I'm only a simple, law-abiding principal. What a wacko that woman must be!

INTEROFFICE MEMO
FROM: Mrs. Rosemary
TO: Principal Floren
I've relayed your message to her. She says that she "knows all about Marianne Cleaver" and how you've "groomed her," but that Mutual will "certainly show you." I told her I had no idea what she meant—which is true, of course.

INTEROFFICE MEMO
FROM: Mrs. Rosemary
TO: Principal Floren
Guess what? Mrs. Scrivener called again. She told me that when Mutual wins the bee, all of your "wicked ways" will be exposed. Next time she calls, can I pretend not to be here?

INTEROFFICE MEMO
FROM: Principal Richard M. Floren
TO: Chrissie Woodward

Please see what you can find out about Mutual's parents—see what they have against Marianne Cleaver and those guys in funny hats who drive the little cars in the parade. Destroy this message. Eat it or something. I'll have Doris in the cafeteria slip you an extra cookie. More memos later.

INTEROFFICE MEMO
FROM: Principal Richard M. Floren
TO: Mrs. Boffin

Have you found out if Mutual is as good a speller as they say?

INTEROFFICE MEMO
FROM: Mrs. Boffin
TO: Principal Floren

I have told you already that I do not know whether Mutual is as good at spelling as "they say." And I have told you all I am going to say on the matter—you can find out for yourself on Bee Day.

INTEROFFICE MEMO
FROM: Principal Floren
TO: Cafeteria staff
I know that the hot lunch today is fried chicken, but I have a terrible craving for hamburgers. Can you please whip some up for me?

INTEROFFICE MEMO
FROM: Mrs. Boffin
TO: Mrs. Rosemary
As a matter of curiosity, why DID we need to hand in a list of names of children who would be taking the written test? The students found it strange, and so did I. Why is Richard so interested in the bee?

INTEROFFICE MEMO
FROM: Mrs. Rosemary
TO: Mrs. Boffin
Once again, I must remind you that, as principal, Richard Floren had every right to request the lists for whatever purpose he felt necessary. I do not know the answer, but it is his own business.
P.S.: Your tone in your memo re: Mutual Scrivener's spelling skills was uncalled for.

INTEROFFICE MEMO
FROM: Principal Richard M. Floren
TO: Chrissie Woodward

Does Mutual ever talk about having "connections" with the governor of Illinois?

INTEROFFICE MEMO
FROM: Principal Richard M. Floren
TO: Chrissie Woodward

Out of curiosity, what would you say the odds are that Harlan can win the bee? I'm thinking ten to one or so. Sound about right?

INTEROFFICE MEMO
FROM: Principal Floren
TO: All staff

At 4 p.m. on Friday, all staff MUST attend the seminar on bee-related conduct. We will discuss how to prepare our students for the bee and how to prepare them for the local reporters who will be covering the event. Attendance is mandatory. Location will be determined at a meeting over lunch today.

9
HARLAN

infamous — adjective. Having an extremely bad reputation. *Walter thought that bringing his collection of scabs to school would make him famous, but it only made him infamous.*

There's this saying I learned from my cousin Brian. It goes, "You might as well be hanged for a sheep as a lamb." It's a really old saying, I think.

I'm not sure how it started, but apparently a long time ago some guy was going to break into a farm and steal a lamb. Then he realized that if they caught him, they'd hang him. So, instead of a little lamb, he decided to steal a big sheep. If he was going to be hanged, he figured he might as well be hanged for something good.

And I kept repeating that phrase to myself over and over while I made my plans for the bee. The spelling bee was such a big deal that anything I did to disrupt it was probably going to get me in major trouble anyway, so I figured I might as well cause a BIG disruption, not a small one.

What I had in mind was going to be no small operation. And as soon as I got it into my head, I knew I'd need your help, Chrissie. The school trusts you—or it did back then, anyway. And you'd be the only person in class who wasn't actually IN the bee, so you'd have a pretty good chance at getting to the mixing boards. I was going to need someone who could mess with the sound system.

So I waited around for you while you followed Mutual out to his car on Wednesday.

Should I call you "you" in this thing? I know that this is really for the school board, right?

Okay.

I waited for *Chrissie Woodward* while *she* followed Mutual out to his car on Wednesday. Then, when she started walking back toward the school, I stepped out from behind the bushes where I'd been hiding. I think I scared the crap out of her for a second there.

"Hey, Chrissie," I said.

"Hey," she said, like she wasn't that glad to see me at all. She looked down at her notebook and tried to just walk past me, but I stepped in front of her and tried to keep talking. This was important stuff.

"Finding out much about Mutual?" I asked.

"Nothing yet," she said. "If you don't mind, I have work to do."

"Hang on a second," I said. "I have something to tell you. It's . . . sort of a secret."

Chrissie stopped in her tracks. I'd planned this whole meeting in my head over the last couple of days, and I knew that if Chrissie didn't seem much like talking, all I really had to do was say something about a secret. She wouldn't be able to resist that.

Sorry, Chrissie, but you have to admit that you're a sucker for secrets.

"What kind of secret?" she asked.

"Follow me around behind the school," I said. "I'll tell you there."

We wandered around behind the school, past the playground, and into this little wooded area that separated the playground from the backyards of a couple of houses. I sat down against a tree, and she sat in front of me, holding out her notebook.

"What's the big secret?" Chrissie asked.

"Well," I said, slowly, "I have a plan for the spelling bee. And I need your help."

"Go on," Chrissie said. She was writing it all down.

"Um." I paused. I had planned all of this out, but actually saying it was sort of different. "It's like . . . well, do you remember when we were in kindergarten?"

Chrissie nodded. "Of course."

"Me too," I said. "And I remember that, my first week there, a bunch of second graders told me about Johnny Dean."

"Everyone knows about Johnny Dean," Chrissie said. "The kid who painted Checkers purple. I'm not helping you kidnap Floren's dog, though."

"I know," I said. "There's no way I'd get away with that now. I mean, ever since the Rubber Band War to End All Rubber Band Wars, the staff hasn't trusted me a bit. But I have bigger plans. Normally you'd be the last person I'd tell about plans ahead of time, but I think you're the only one who can really help."

"You should have been in a lot more trouble for that," she said. "Jake got in more trouble than you did, you know?"

"Did he really?" I said. "I didn't know. Should I say something to Floren about it?"

I really didn't know Jake had been in trouble over the rubber band war. He wasn't even involved in it!

"No point," said Chrissie. "He won't get you in trouble over anything this close to the bee."

I made up my mind to apologize to Jake next time I saw him.

"Anyway," I said, "this is my last semester here. I've pulled some good jokes and all of that, but nothing that anyone's going to tell the kindergartners about next year, let alone three or four years from now. The bee is my last chance to really leave my mark."

"So what's the plan?" she asked.

"First of all, I'm going to break into the top five of the bee."

"So you can go to districts?"

"Nah. I just want to make the top five so that everyone will be paying attention. Every kid knows that their teachers are going to make them look up every word that comes up at the end of the bee, right? So I'll have everyone's undivided attention."

"So what do you want to do?" asked Chrissie.

"When it gets to be my turn, I'm going to step to the microphone and burp."

"Burp?"

"Yep." I smiled proudly. "Anyone can burp on command, but I've been practicing. I can let out a really, really good belch whenever I want. Wanna see?"

"No," she said. "I believe you. That's your whole plan? You're going to burp?"

"Not just any burp—a belch to end all belches."

"And what do I have to do with it?"

"You won't be in the bee. You'll be out in the audience. And they trust you. Do you think you can manage to sit behind the sound booth?"

"Probably."

"I'll give you a signal right before I burp, and you can jump in and turn up the volume on the microphone. I can get a good reaction just by burping into the mike, but if the volume is turned way up . . . I can shake the windows and rattle the walls. People will remember it forever! And it'll be on TV, so the whole TOWN will see it! And then the clip will spread all over the world, I'll bet!"

She stared at me for a minute.

"How do you know I'm not going to turn you in for this?" she asked.

"I thought of that," I said. "The way I see it, you can't turn me in for planning to burp. There's no rule against it. I checked the school rule books and the official spelling bee rules, and there's not one thing about burping in either of them. The worst you could do is spoil the surprise."

"I guess," she said.

I really did look that up. It's true. There's no way you can get in trouble for suspicion of planning to belch, even if you're planning a really, really big one. If you actually *do* belch over and over and over again, they might be able to get you for disrupting the class, but that's about it. This is the best kind of prank—the kind you can't actually get in trouble for. All the best class clowns do their homework. That's how I knew that I wouldn't get in trouble for bringing a goat to school—there was no rule against it.

But it was still a risk. Just because there isn't a rule saying you can't do something doesn't mean they won't punish you anyway. Sometimes they make rules up as they go along. You know that song "Mary Had a Little Lamb"? It says that the lamb "followed her to school one day, which was against the rules." I'll bet anything there wasn't actually a rule on the books about letting a lamb follow you to school, but Mary still got in trouble. She might as well have brought a big sheep to school instead.

Anyway, I was pretty sure they wouldn't try to go after me for a single belch. Even a big one. And the worst they could possibly give me was detention until I was out of Gordon Liddy Community School. That was only a few months. Being a legend is worth that kind of time.

"So what do you say? Can you help me out?"

Chrissie looked at the ground for a couple of seconds while she thought it over.

"Maybe," she said.

I knew I was asking a lot of her. She was all about law and order, and I was asking her to help really cause a disruption. It wasn't her style. I should have offered her cash or something.

So that's what really happened. I know someone told the school board they saw us having a secret meeting that day, and that they thought I was asking Chrissie to help me cheat. But that's just not true. All I was doing was asking her to help me become a legend.

10
MUTUAL

rhapsodic—adjective. Joyfully enthusiastic or ecstatic. *Members of the Good Times Gang sang in rhapsodic tones about nutrition.*

By Thursday, my third day at Gordon Liddy Community School, my curiosity as to what a band of demons on motorcycles would sound like was killing me. I assumed that they would be loud, of course, but that was all I could imagine. Perhaps they screamed. Perhaps they made you want to do bad things. My parents always said that rock music tricked people into setting fires.

That morning, Mother came in to wake me up at seven o'clock, but I had already been awake for hours. While I ate my breakfast, she had me do several words, including "jasmine," "vestibule," "defenestration," and "sarsaparilla." I spelled them all correctly, of course, but I was not thinking of spelling.

When I first arrived in class that morning, nobody else was there. This was quite possibly the first time I had ever been in a room outside my house all by myself, but I did not think much about that at the time. I simply took my seat and began to study my dictionary.

A minute later, Marianne Cleaver entered the room.

"Good morning, Marianne," I said.

She paused at her desk and stared at me. "No time to talk," she said. "Time spent talking is time wasted."

"Do you study a lot at home?" I asked.

She pulled a very large dictionary out of her backpack. "More than you do, I'll bet," she said. "If you think you're going to beat me, you've got another think coming, Mutual Scrivener. You call *that* a dictionary?"

She pointed to the book on my desk, and I nodded.

"Well," she snorted, "you'll never be able to learn all the words you need to know out of a flimsy little thing like that! What is it, a picture dictionary for second graders?"

"It is just a regular dictionary," I said. "Just like any other."

She held hers up triumphantly. "No," she said, "*this* is a regular dictionary. Over three thousand pages. You're dead meat at the bee!"

And she sat down and began to study.

I was a bit doubtful as to my parents' claims that all of the other students were corrupt, but it was certainly true in Marianne Cleaver's case.

Slowly, the other students began to arrive. Jennifer came in, holding a large book of Shakespeare plays. I tried to say hello to her, but no words came out.

Jason and Amber came in at the same time, and sat down in the seats next to mine.

"Hello," I said.

"Hey, man," Jason said. "How's it going?"

"All right," I said.

"Getting any more corrupt?" Amber asked. She may have been making fun of me, in a way, but she was being much more pleasant than Marianne had been.

"Not yet," I said. I looked at Jason's shirt, which, like his shirt from the day before, had the logo for Paranormal Execution, only this time it was over a picture of a man in a hooded cloak holding a lantern. I decided that it could not hurt to learn more about the music. The man with the lantern did not look evil, after all. He looked wise.

And I decided that, if I wanted to be attractive to people like Jennifer, I would have to learn more of the outside world. I knew nothing of popular culture.

"Would it be too much trouble," I asked, "if I were to ask you to let me hear Paranormal Execution?"

Jason smiled. "You wanna hear some metal?" he asked.

"I would like to," I said. "But only if it will not make me want to start fires or kill my parents."

Amber laughed. "Who told you it would do that?" she asked.

"My parents," I told her.

She laughed again. "You'd have to be pretty unstable to start with to let a song convince you to kill someone."

"Are the men who sing metal popular with girls?" I asked.

"Are you kidding?" Jason said. "Rock singers can be the ugliest, dumbest guys on the planet, and they'll still get all the girls."

"I see," I said. "But it will not MAKE me stupid, right?"

"Don't worry about it," Jason said. "Just follow us at re-cess." He patted his backpack, which I suppose meant that it contained some of the music. "And we'll have you head-banging in no time."

"Will it hurt?" I asked.

Jason and Amber laughed, and Jason shook his head. "Trust me," he said. "You'll be fine. We won't let you get hurt."

It was nice to have friends looking out for my welfare, even if they were corrupt.

When recess finally arrived, I followed Jason and Amber outside. Jason took his backpack along, and they led me over to an area around the corner of the school where no one from the playground could see us. I had rarely been so nervous in my life.

"Are we allowed to be here?" I asked. "There is no adult supervision!"

"It's fine," said Jason, smiling.

I noticed a cigarette butt sitting on the ground. "Someone has been smoking here," I said.

"It's probably one of the teachers," said Amber. "Most of them smoke."

My parents would certainly not be surprised to hear this.

"Anyway," said Jason, pulling something out of his back-pack. "We'll start you off on a slow one. Put these on."

He handed me a pair of headphones, and I put them onto my head.

"Not too loud, please," I said.

He smiled. He pushed a button on a little machine that the headphones were connected to, and a second later there was a tremendous noise in my ears, so loud and scary that I nearly threw the headphones from my head.

Then it slowed down, so that for just a second there was a single electrical guitar playing, just like a campfire song, but then the noisier instruments started again, and a voice started singing something about infinity.

I had never heard anything like it. It got faster and then slower again, then fast, and when the man was done singing, one of the players played a solo that sounded like a weather machine malfunctioning, or a cat screaming, only there was a bit of a melody behind it. It sounded as though it was expressing anger, or fear, or something like that. I had certainly never heard music that was able to do that before. It was terrifying—but exciting at the same time. It made me feel as though I were going on an epic journey into space or into far-off lands. I did not know that music could do that.

Jason watched my face as I listened to the song all the way through.

"What do you think?" he asked as it finished.

I took a deep breath and thought about what I'd heard. I had listened to a whole heavy-metal song, and I did not feel at all inclined to take drugs, commit crimes, or burn things. Maybe the song had not worked, or maybe I was just too strong to be taken in by their tricks.

"More, please," I said.

Jason and Amber smiled.

11
JENNIFER

pathological—adjective. Uncontrolled or unreasonable. *A flood in my uncle Henry's basement led to his pathological obsession with checking for leaks in the plumbing.*

I loved, loved, LOVED the None of the Above school of studying. All I did was read Shakespeare and look up the stuff I didn't know—not just the words, but the history and all of that. At the bottom of every page of the Shakespeare book, there were notes on that sort of stuff. For the first time in my life, I really felt like I was actually getting smarter, not just making myself look better to colleges. And I was feeling more relaxed than I ever had. I don't know what it is about reading Shakespeare, but it just makes me breathe better. Weird, huh?

Look, it's like this: I have this idea in my head for the kind of person I want to be. The kind you sometimes see in movies or read about. They have their own cool way of living that seems strange at first, but turns out to make perfect sense. Some people think they're nuts, but they're actually really smart. That's what I want to be. One of those sorts of people.

It was one reason for me to want to win the bee. Not only would Mutual be impressed with me, but when people came up and asked me how I'd done it, I'd surprise them all by telling them about the None of the Above school of studying. And they'd all say "What a fascinating person!"

On the other hand, I was getting more and more afraid of what was going to happen if I DIDN'T win. At the very least, my parents would think they had to sign me up for even MORE activities. Military school probably wasn't out of the question. But if I won, Mom could probably talk Dad into letting me drop a few of them altogether.

Anyway, by midweek, Marianne had mostly stopped speaking in multiple-choice questions. Instead she was spelling at least one word out of every sentence she uttered. Like, she'd say "What did you bring for L-U-N-C-H today?" or "Don't you wish that the school would start up a K-A-Y-A-K-I-N-G club?" Maybe she actually *was* learning two letters' worth of words per night—in fact, I hoped she was. It would be a shame for her to look as stressed and miserable as she did for nothing.

But she wasn't the only one who was starting to freak out. Every time I passed Amber in the halls, it seemed like she was chanting something under her breath, or staring intently at her pencil, like she was trying to get it to move with only the power of her mind. If she and Jason hadn't had Mutual, the new kid, to keep them busy, she might have gotten herself stuck in some sort of trance.

Even Tony Ostanek, who normally only read video

game magazines, was reading the dictionary during SSR. And rumor had it that you were up to two notebooks a day, with college-ruled lines, Chrissie.

The only person who didn't seem to be acting strange was Mutual. I guess I don't know how he normally acted, but he reminded me of a cat who was just getting to explore the backyard for the first time. He looked at everything like it was new and fascinating.

But I wasn't getting anywhere with him. He hadn't asked me about *Henry V* again, and he was always talking to Jason and Amber, so I never really had a chance to go up and talk to him. But I was reading *Henry V*, and I planned to ask him about it the first chance I got. Maybe if I won the bee, he'd want to try None of the Above studying with me.

At lunch on Thursday, I sat at my usual spot, next to Jake. Sitting near him is sort of a dangerous habit, because you never knew when he could be called upon to eat something gross for a dollar. Jake's a nice guy, though. And when I want to just sit there and ramble about Shakespeare out loud, he doesn't mind, and he never acts like I'm nuts. Still, even though eating for dollars interests me more than most sports, I don't really need a front-row seat.

Sure enough, I was just finishing my sandwich—thank goodness—when Tony Ostanek, Harlan Sturr, and Gunther Vredenberg showed up, holding a Baggie full of something that looked suspiciously like barf.

"Hey, Chow!" said Tony. "Look what we've got!"

"What is it?" asked Jake, whose mouth was still full of shoestring potatoes.

"It's a little bit of everything," said Tony. "A peanut

butter and jelly sandwich, some blueberry yogurt, and milk, all mixed together. Here you go!" He dropped the disgusting bag onto the table in front of Jake, along with a dollar.

"Go, Chow, go!" said Harlan. Then the others joined in, chanting, "Go, Chow, go!" The other kids at the table took the cue, and pretty soon the whole long table was shouting, "Go, Chow, go!"

I couldn't look—I turned my head away and closed my eyes really tight so I wouldn't have to watch if he actually ate the stuff. And I knew he would. Sure enough, after about ten seconds, everyone quit chanting and started cheering. I looked back up to see Jake holding up the empty Baggie with one hand and the dollar bill in the other, grinning triumphantly.

When all the cheering died down, he was still smiling.

"That was really gross, Jake," I said.

He shrugged. "It wasn't so bad. I mean, peanut butter, jelly, yogurt . . . all good stuff. And I can always use an extra buck."

He went back to the shoestring potatoes he'd packed with his lunch.

"But aren't you worried that one day you'll eat something that makes you sick?"

"Heck no! My mom never disinfected anything when I was a kid."

"So?"

"So I built up an immune system that can't be beat!" he said. "It's great! It's probably a more useful thing to have than anything they teach you in school."

It kind of freaked me out that Jake's mom, who

happened to be the lunch lady, didn't disinfect things at home, but saying so wouldn't have been too polite.

"You have a point there," I said. "Very rarely will knowing how to spell some disease actually keep you from getting it."

"But I still want to win the bee," he said. "At Hedekker's Appliance Store, they have this awesome set of nonstick cookware for seventy-five dollars. That's what I'd get if I won the gift certificate!"

"You know, Jake, you may be the first person ever to enter the all-school bee for the prizes."

He grinned, then stood up to throw out his trash, and promptly stepped on a banana peel.

My dad always says that there are two kinds of losers in the world. The first is the kind who can't walk across the room holding a bowl of soup without spilling it. The other kind is the guy he spills the soup on. I'm not sure that getting soup spilled on you really makes you a loser—unlucky is a better word—but that's Jake, all right. Everything always happens to him. If a meteor crashed through the roof of the school, it would surely be his desk that it destroyed.

For instance, after Harlan Sturr's attempt to start the Rubber Band War to End All Rubber Band Wars, the school added rubber bands to their list of objects that violated the school's zero-tolerance weapons policy, which meant that you could get suspended for being caught with rubber bands. And poor Jake was the first person to be caught with one. It wasn't even a weapon, either—he was just using it to hold plastic wrap over a couple of broccoli crowns that he brought with his lunch. But he got in trouble, anyway.

One thing I'll say for Jake—he took it all in stride. And he seemed to have his life pretty well figured out. He knew what he was good at, and he stuck with it. I suppose there's no shame in that. At least he wasn't letting the stress from the spelling bee get to him, like it was doing to lots of other kids. He walked around grinning most of the time.

But the person who seemed most stressed about the bee wasn't a student at all—it was my father. And, for some reason, he had no confidence that I could win it without cheating, which was pretty annoying, because I totally could. But I guess no one worries about hurting a new kind of cola's feelings, right?

When Dad came home from work on Thursday night, he showed me the new outfit he'd bought—a black turtleneck with black pants and a black ski mask.

"It's perfect!" he said, holding it up proudly. "It's what all the guys who break into buildings wear!"

"Don't you think it'll look suspicious?" I asked. "I mean, if anyone sees you in the school wearing something like that, they'll know right away that you're up to no good."

"Honey," he said, "leave this to me. I know how to sneak into buildings, okay? They taught me a few tricks when I was in military school."

"They taught you how to break into buildings?" I asked.

"Not exactly," he said. "But they taught me some things that I'm sure can be applied to this sort of job. You learn very practical things there."

"Dad, I'm begging you," I said. "I can win the bee without the word list. Please don't break into the school."

Just then, the phone rang, and he went to answer it.

He talked on the phone to somebody for a long time—like, twenty minutes. I couldn't make out what he was saying at all, because he was more mumbling than talking. But every now and then he would poke his head into the room and give me a thumbs-up. Finally he said, "Thank you, sir," and hung up.

"Don't worry, honey," he said. "I've just made arrangements that will keep me out of trouble. The break-in is on for tomorrow!"

"Who was that on the phone?" I asked.

"No one," he said. "No one at all."

I sat in my room thinking for a long time after this. Dad was actually going to break into the school and try to make me cheat. I didn't even need to cheat—I was feeling like I was going to do fine on my own.

It made me really, really nervous to know that some creep out there wanted me to win badly enough to help Dad break into the school. What did anyone else care if I won? Was he bribing someone? It was enough to make me lose the bee on purpose, just so that that person didn't get what they wanted.

In fact, I had almost made up my mind to lose on purpose when I crept downstairs for a midnight snack. I happened to look down at Dad's desk and saw that there was a brochure sitting around for a place called Orthogonian Academy. A military school. And he had circled a section about how attractive Orthogonian graduates were to colleges.

I took the brochure up to my room and tore it into tiny little pieces, but I knew that if Dad was set on me going there, he could always get another brochure. If I didn't want to go there, I'd probably have to win that bee.

But I couldn't let him break into the school, one way or the other. One of us had to be the sane one in the house, and it sure wasn't going to be him. And I didn't know how to stop him, but I knew someone who would.

You, Chrissie.

12
JAKE

okra — noun. A slimy green vegetable common in the southeastern United States. *Paul refused to eat okra on the grounds that it "looked way too much like snot."*

Most people think I'm not that smart. I guess I kinda see why. People see me in the cafeteria eating bags of bread mixed with yogurt and stuff, and they think, *How smart can a person who eats stuff for dollars be?*

But it's all a secret plan, ha ha.

You see, I want to be a chef. And being the lunch lady's son might seem like a good place to start, but it isn't. Not if you want to be a *great* chef.

In big cities, chefs don't just make sloppy joes and hot dogs and Salisbury steak. The really popular chefs make really weird stuff, like swordfish with grape jelly. And then they charge, like, a hundred dollars for it. They talk about it on the food shows on TV all the time. I watch them every day. I may not get very good grades, but if cooking were a subject, I'd probably do a lot better!

I stay after school every day while Mom cleans up the kitchen and starts cooking the food for the next day. Usually I just hang around in the gym shooting baskets. Sometimes Floren comes in and bets me a handful of cookies that he can make more baskets than me, and I always win. If I ever get really fat, it will probably be Principal Floren's fault. He's kind of a jerk, you know. He got me in trouble just for bringing a rubber band to lunch one day. Even Harlan eventually apologized to me when he heard about it, since he was the one who really should have been in trouble.

On days when Floren isn't around to shoot baskets, I hang out in the kitchen. I'll bet I know everything you can learn about cooking from a school cafeteria. But that isn't much. I can't learn about swordfish and grape jelly from there, ha ha!

But every day, some kid gives me something weird to try, and pays me a dollar for it. And maybe one day I'll discover a great new flavor from it. And then I'll become a chef and serve it to people and charge them a hundred dollars for something people used to pay ME to eat. Most of the great food discoveries have probably been accidents made by regular people. Like, the guy who first put chocolate and peanut butter together was probably just some guy who was down to nothing but a candy bar and some peanut butter in his pantry and mixed them up. And he probably won a Nobel Prize! Or, if he didn't, I think he should have.

And that's why I entered the bee. They have some very fine cookware for sale at Hedekker's Appliance Store, you know. If I get it, then I can cook better things at home. Mom doesn't cook food at school because she loves to cook, ha ha. When she gets home, she doesn't feel much like cooking anymore. It's sort of like how Mr. Ruggles, the janitor, probably never mops his own floor.

And I'm not that bad at spelling. You just kind of have to think of things like the recipe for a word. That's what I do. Judging by my spelling grades, it works about seventy percent of the time, ha ha!

I know I'm not as smart as Marianne or Jennifer, but I'm not stupid. And sometimes I think my mom thinks I am. Because she never seems surprised when my grades aren't good. She always tells me to do my best, but sometimes I think she maybe thinks my best is only B-minus work. Maybe because that's the best grade I ever get, ha ha.

But just watch. In fifteen years, when people come into my restaurant, I'll bet they won't say, "That chef has trouble retaining what he learns about long division." They will say, "That chef is a genius."

13
CHRISSIE

Excerpt from notebook #40:
Jennifer's dad drives a red car with a "My Daughter Is an Honor Student at State" bumper sticker on it. Probably about Val.

I had advance word about the break-in, as everyone knows. But I wasn't the only one. I made sure of that.

Jennifer told me everything she knew first thing Friday morning and begged me to stop it from happening. I told her I'd do whatever I could.

So I wrote a memo to Floren suggesting that there was a rumored break-in that night, and they might want security to be tight around the office. I put it in a sealed envelope and gave it to Mrs. Boffin to deliver to him.

In a way, giving him the memo was like giving him one last chance to prove that I could trust him to do the right thing. But I never heard back from him. Not even a thank-you memo and an offer of an extra cookie.

I officially no longer trusted him. In fact, I was starting to think something fishy was going on in regard to the bee.

Maybe the reason he never responded was that he was involved! Or, anyway, maybe someone in the office was. And I was going to find out what was going on and get anyone involved fired.

My whole world was upside down. I was starting to investigate the school instead of the students, and I was actually considering helping Harlan with a prank rather than turning him in. Even though I'd gotten Harlan in trouble many times, I did sort of respect him. You sort of have to take your hat off to a kid who knows as many verses to "Diarrhea Cha Cha Cha" as Harlan does. And I know that he apologized to Jake about the rubber band incident as soon as I told him about it, which was really nice of him. And it was probably true that he couldn't get in trouble just for planning to burp. In fact, there's no way he'd get in trouble if he did it, because if he was in the top five, he'd be going to districts. People going to districts are treated like heroes—he could probably shout a swearword into the mike and get away with it if he was in the top five. But the very fact that I was considering helping him with, instead of turning him in for, the prank he had in mind felt very strange indeed.

Then, on Friday, things got even stranger.

There I was, standing at the edge of the playground, when I heard someone calling my name. I turned around to see a couple of old ladies standing at the other end of the wooded area, by the street. I recognized them, of course—I recognize everyone in Preston. They were the two old ladies that I sometimes saw sitting in the Burger Baron, shouting at each other—I'd sort of always wanted more data on them. I walked over to them very slowly.

"Hello, Chrissie," said one of them. She sounded as sweet as honey, but she was looking at me like a spider at a fly.

I pride myself on never being afraid, but I have to admit, there was something scary about these old ladies, and the "sweet" voice only made them scarier. What were they doing on school property? They weren't allowed without a visitor pass. Were they going to kidnap me? I've heard stories about old ladies who kidnap girls and make them be their new granddaughter. Any minute one of them could have held a chloroformed hankie up to my nose, and when I woke up, I'd be in some old house full of doilies and appliances they'd ordered off of the Home Shopping channel. They'd make me wear frilly dresses, bake banana nut bread, and watch beauty pageants. Naturally, every good detective is trained in self-defense, but I couldn't very well attack old ladies, now, could I? The school puts a lot of trust in me, but if I used a roundhouse kick to break an old lady's hip, I doubt they'd believe it was self-defense.

"Hello," I said, nervously.

"Relax, dear," said one of them. "We just want to ask you some questions."

"That's right," said the other. "Just some questions."

I've seen enough cop movies to know perfectly well that absolutely everyone who says "We just want to ask you some questions" is up to something.

"Shut up, Agnes!" said the first one. "I already told her that!"

"Can it, Helen, you old ninny!" said the other one, Agnes. "I'm trying to be reassuring!"

"Well, you're doing a lousy job of it!" said the first one, Helen.

"Ladies!" I said. "Settle down!" They stopped shouting, and Helen reared her head back and hawked a loogey, which landed square on one of the trees. It was among the most disgusting things I've ever seen, and I've been watching Jake Wells eat things for dollars in the cafeteria since I was six.

"Nice shot," said Agnes.

"Thank you," said Helen. Then Agnes handed her a dollar, which she put in her pocket.

It was then that I knew it for sure: I was dealing with a couple of kooks.

"We want to know about Mutual Scrivener," said Helen.

"Get in line," I snapped. I know I'm supposed to be courteous to my elders and all, but you sacrifice some courtesy when you hawk a loogey in front of someone. "I don't know much."

It wasn't that unusual for people to come up to me and ask me who I thought was going to win the bee. In fact, every time I went anywhere with my parents, SOME old person who was all excited about the bee would come up and ask me questions. But this was the first time anyone had come up to me during the school day like that. And the first time I'd seen old people spit so much.

"Is he as good of a speller as people say he is?" asked Helen.

"I think so," I said.

"But is he studying good and hard, like he should be?" asked Agnes.

94

"I don't know about what he does at home," I said. "But he's not studying much at school anymore. He spends most of his time talking about heavy-metal bands now."

Helen spit on the ground. Agnes whacked her in the arm with a purse.

"Ouch!" Helen shouted. "That hurt!"

"That's the idea, you ninny!" shouted Agnes.

Agnes started snorting, like she was getting ready to hawk a loogey, too. And a good one. You don't have Harlan in your class for years without learning the sound of a good loogey in the works.

I turned around and ran as fast as I could. I knew I had to get away before they started spitting at each other instead of trees. They'd be spitting at me next.

When I turned back to look at them again, they were nowhere to be seen.

Things were getting stranger and stranger, all right.

But with a break-in about to happen that night, old ladies seemed like the least of my concerns. They were probably just two of the many old people in town who seemed like the only thing keeping them alive was their devotion to Gordon Liddy Community School's spelling program.

14

Jason—

Did you see those old ladies on the playground? You should've done something to freak them out! Mutual's never seen you in action.

—Amber

Amber—

Yeah. I was busy continuing Mutual's "education." Where were you?

—Jason

I was in the tree. You can make spells more powerful by being close to nature, so I climbed up it to cast a certain kind of spell.

—A

What kind?

—J

It's a secret!

—A

Okay. Maybe I'll ask Chrissie Woodward!

—J

That's who the old ladies were talking to. I saw the whole thing from up in the tree. One of them came THIS CLOSE to spitting on me. It was nasty!
—A

Ew! What were they talking to Chrissie about?
—J

About Mutual. That's why I'm writing. Don't wanna freak him out. But they were really interested in whether he's going to do well at the bee. I think they may be out to get him.
—A

Well, we'll have to protect him, won't we? Don't worry. No old ladies bug my friends on my watch!
—J

15
MUTUAL

kyoodle—verb. To make loud, useless noises. *"I like nice songs about rivers and huckleberries,"* said Grandma Pat. *"All those rock bands ever do is kyoodle!"*

Jason loaned me a device that would allow me to listen to the music of Paranormal Execution at home over the weekend—with headphones, so my parents would not know. I wanted to learn more of their music, now that I had learned that rock music was not just loud, dangerous noise, and he was happy to help. I knew that Jason and Amber were corrupt—Jason talked frequently about things that he had done to frighten his elders—but, for corrupt troublemakers, they were very nice. And Amber had promised not to curse me on the day of the spelling bee, so it was lucky for me that I had made friends with them.

I was still studying hard for the bee, but often, when I appeared to be reading a dictionary, I was actually very sneakily looking at the covers of the Paranormal Execution albums, which I had slipped into the dictionary. One showed rows and rows of gravestones with lightning bolts and ghostly men in Civil War uniforms. Another showed several men pointing at the camera and sneering—from the pictures Jason showed me of other heavy-metal bands, it was clear that they were all very much in the habit of pointing at cameras and sneering. But I did not see any harm in that. Sneers do not hurt anyone.

I was still spending every minute of my time in the library reading about Shakespeare, but I could not get the nerve to talk to Jennifer about it. She would probably ignore me again. Perhaps if I became more knowledgeable about Shakespeare and rock music, and then won the spelling bee, she would be impressed.

At the end of the day, Jason recommended two or three Paranormal Execution songs that I might especially enjoy, patted me on the back, and told me to have a good day. Amber wiggled her fingers in my face, spun around, and said that she had just given me good luck. I imagined that my parents would think that this witchcraft was very bad, but how could giving someone good luck be bad?

As I was walking down the hallway, I was approached by Mrs. Rosemary.

"Hi, Mutual!" she said. "Principal Floren would like to speak with you for a moment!"

"I need to get to my parents, or they will worry," I said. This was true, but the real reason I wanted to leave was that I was anxious to get home and listen to music on the headphones while I studied.

"Oh, it will only be for a second," said Mrs. Rosemary. "He just needs to see how you're doing."

"All right." I nodded. She was smiling so brightly that I could not say no to her, though I was slightly afraid that she would pull a muscle in her cheeks. She would certainly be sore in the morning.

She led me into the office, then pointed into a room in the office where Principal Floren was sitting at his desk.

"Mr. Scrivener!" he said happily. "Come in. Take a seat."

I walked in and sat in front of his desk. Few, if any, people had ever called me mister before, but I took it as a sign of respect.

"How are you enjoying your time here at Gordon Liddy?" he asked.

"Oh, it is very nice," I said. "I am learning a lot."

"Wonderful!" he said. "One of my top priorities is creating a positive learning environment for all of our students."

"And next week will be the spelling bee," I said.

"Precisely what I wanted to talk to you about!" he said, smiling. "Are you a good speller, Mutual?"

"Give me a word," I said. "Give me any word, and I'll do it."

"Really?" he said. "All right . . . how about . . . 'sinister'?"

"Sinister," I said. "Adjective. Evil or corrupt. Also Latin for left-handed. The reporters uncovered the president's sinister plan. S-I-N-I-S-T-E-R. Sinister."

He nodded. "Very impressive, Mr. Scrivener. But I'm a little bit concerned, because all of the other students have been here so much longer—it seems like they may have an unfair advantage over you. Some people have suggested to me that you may need help to keep the contest even."

"I believe I will be all right," I said.

"Just the same," said Principal Floren, "it's a long-standing policy of ours to make sure that new students don't have a disadvantage, because we want the spelling bee to have a perfectly level playing field. Many of the words on the master word list are words that we know they've had in spelling classes since they were in second grade, after all."

I nodded. "Yes, sir," I said.

"You don't have to call me sir," he said. "Just 'Principal' is fine. Anyway, to make sure you have a fair shot, I want to give you this list of words." He handed me a handwritten sheet of several words, none of which were matched with a definition or part of speech.

"Thank you," I said, taking it, "but are you sure that this is moral?"

"I just want to make sure the spelling bee is fair," he said. "As long as the principal is doing something, it's moral. But just in case anyone thinks that it isn't fair for you to have the same advantages that the other students had, I need you to keep this top secret. You can't tell anyone about this. Not even your parents or your friends. Memorize the list, then destroy it. Do you understand?"

"Yes, Principal Floren," I said.

"Good, Mr. Scrivener. Sometimes we have to do things secretly—it's one of the executive privileges that come with being the principal," he said. "Now be careful!"

I told him I would, and got up to leave.

When I arrived at the car, my parents were nearly in hysterics.

"Where have you been?" Mother asked. "Most of the

other children have already gone home! We were afraid you had been kidnapped! Or killed!"

"Nothing is wrong, Mother," I said. "Principal Floren asked me to stay a couple of extra minutes."

"Keeping children after school!" said Mother. "That can hardly even be legal, can it, Norm?"

"No," said Father. "Not legal."

"That is what Jason says about keeping people after school for detention," I said.

"Detention, eh?" asked Mother. "Is that what they do to troublemakers around here?"

"Yes," I said.

"So that is what happened, then?" she said. "He gave you a detention? Well, Mutual, do not feel bad. People are going to persecute you for being different. They have never met someone as moral or germ-free as you, and they will surely want to punish you for it. That is the way the world works."

"No one has persecuted me for being moral," I said.

"That is what they are making it look like, Mutual," she said. "But I know better. I know their tricks and manners."

"But Principal Floren did not give me detention," I said. "He only wanted to make sure I was able to spell well enough to be in the bee."

"Well, then, I expect you certainly showed him," she said. "They think that just because we have not let them get their hooks into you, you must not be able to spell anything. Well, they will be in for a surprise next week!"

That night, I sat alone in my room, listening to Paranormal Execution. This was the first time I had listened to an entire album all at once—I liked the way they paced it so the first song was fast, then the next was slower. The songs all sort of flowed together. It would make me feel excited, then give me a chance to recover. Some songs made me feel as though I were marching into battle, and some made me feel as though I were in a little medieval village, relaxing after a long day of hunting for dragons.

Also, for the first time, I was able to understand the words. I had always heard that rock musicians were not smart, but the songs I heard used lots of words that indicated that the person who wrote them had a fine vocabulary. Like in my favorite song, "Obfuscate."

> Between the trees of a malodorous swamp
> Hidden far from sight
> Under a veil of mist and fog
> I obfuscate by night

I actually had to look up two of those words. "Obfuscate" means "to cover up or hide." "Malodorous" means "stinky." In any case, I did not see how hiding in a stinky swamp was such a corruptive influence. If I ever find myself in a stinky swamp, I shall also wish to obfuscate. If one does not obfuscate in the swamp at night, one might be discovered by a hungry alligator.

If these words were indeed in common usage in the "outside world," then perhaps I really was at an unfair disadvantage. I had never heard of these words at all—my parents certainly did not use them.

I was so caught up in listening to the music that I did

not even glance at the list of words Principal Floren had given me until late at night. When I finally did look at it, I found that it was a list of sloppily handwritten words—and all of them were words that I knew perfectly well how to spell. I did not look at it very carefully. Since it was all words that I knew, and since the handwriting was very hard to read, I simply put it into a drawer on my desk. I appreciated that the school wished to give me extra help, but it was not necessary.

If Chrissie had not found out about it, I believe that I would have forgotten about the list altogether.

16
CHRISSIE

Excerpt from notebook #5:
Principal Floren can never figure out how to operate gadgets or computers by himself. Mrs. Rosemary does most of that stuff for him.

The last memo I ever sent to Principal Floren was right after lunch on Friday—it was a warning that there were old ladies around, and that they were up to no good. I never heard back from him, of course. And, even though I kept waiting all day, hoping he'd do SOMETHING to make me trust him again, I never got a note back from him regarding the warning about the break-in, either.

Obviously, it was up to me.

I waited in my favorite hiding place in the bushes after school, just watching the front door. I knew that since it was Friday, the only people in the office would be Principal Floren and Mrs. Rosemary. All the teachers left early on Friday. And Floren and Mrs. Rosemary would be leaving early to set up the meeting they were having with the teachers to talk about how to prepare students to deal with the press at the bee. They were holding it at a restaurant in town, but I wasn't sure which one, or I'd have shown up to spy on them.

Mutual was the last one out the door that day, which I thought was strange. He'd been the first one out every other day since he'd come to Gordon Liddy. When he got to his car, his parents looked like they were in hysterics. It would have been a perfect day to hide near the car and find out more about them, but I had too much to do. Investigating the school was more important than investigating other students.

Ten minutes after Mutual left, Mrs. Rosemary came out, smiling as usual. Sometimes I think that when she was a kid, something must have made her smile for so long that her face got stuck that way. Those stories parents tell about that sort of thing aren't true, of course, but it might work for freaks of nature like Mrs. Rosemary.

Five minutes later, Principal Floren walked out, whistling a tune I didn't recognize. I knew that he only whistled when he was nervous, though, so I suspected that something fishy was indeed going on.

Once his car was out of the parking lot, it was time to make my move. I walked into the front door and headed to the office, fingering the lock-picking kit that I had in my pocket.

But, to my surprise, the door wasn't locked at all.

I walked right in, unlocked the padlock on the filing cabinet, and pulled out the copy of the master word list. I was just about to make a run for it when I noticed that there was a video camera set up in Principal Floren's office—and it was running. Surveillance! They were doing a better job of security than I thought! I was a bit surprised that Floren could even use the recorder—technology isn't his strong point.

But it looked like he could use the camera, all right. There was a shelf behind his desk covered in discs labeled things like "Monday morning—9 a.m. till noon" and "Tuesday—written test." Apparently he'd been recording things the whole week!

The camera would have caught me breaking in, so I turned it off, took out the disc, and put it into my bag with the word list. Before I left, I grabbed a blank disc off a pile on Floren's desk to put in the camera, so they wouldn't notice that one was missing until they played it back.

I crept back out as though everything was normal—no one would have suspected anything if they saw me, since I often stayed late anyway. With the recording and the master word list safely in my backpack, I walked home and headed up to my room.

There I watched the disc I'd taken out of the recorder, and saw the footage of what had gone on before I went in. I couldn't believe what I saw. Floren, the guy I actually, for some stupid reason, used to trust, was giving Mutual a copy of the master word list!

Something was going on, all right! And Principal Floren was in on it! The way he was talking to Mutual, Mutual probably wouldn't even realize that he was cheating by looking at that list.

Apparently Principal Floren wanted Mutual to win the bee, for some reason. Otherwise, why would he have given him a copy of the word list?

And someone ELSE wanted Jennifer to win—enough that they were somehow helping her dad break into the school.

Maybe the old ladies from the playground were involved—they seemed to want Mutual to win, too.

I still had a lot to find out. What did Floren care who won? Who called Jennifer's dad?

Maybe it was Mrs. Boffin. Maybe she was in league with the old ladies—they were just about her age. And it made sense that she'd want one of the kids who had been her students all along to beat Mutual—it would make her look bad if some kid who just blew in from homeschooling beat every last one of the kids she'd taught all year.

At the time, I had a framed picture of myself with Floren in the office on my desk. I'd been thinking of getting rid of it for a long time, but that was the afternoon that I finally put it in the trash. I guess I thought I'd be really depressed when I finally dropped it into my garbage can, but I was mostly just relieved, like a weight was off my back. I was still depressed, but mostly depressed that I'd been wrong about him all those years. It felt good to know that I was starting to do what I should have been doing all along. Better late than never.

That night, after dinner, I walked back up to the school to see if anything had happened and try to find more clues. When I got there, Officer Beadle was putting police tape around a broken window. The break-in had happened, all right.

"Jim!" I shouted.

Officer Beadle looked up from his work. "Hey, Chrissie!" he said. "Might've known you'd be swinging by."

"What happened?"

"Just what you said was going to happen, kid," he said. "You did the right thing by telling us." He put down the tape for a second and picked up his thermos, which had been sitting in the snow, and took a sip.

"Did you get any messages from the school saying something was going to happen tonight?"

"Nope." He shook his head.

"Didn't think so," I said. "So what happened, exactly?"

"We saw a guy all dressed in black crawling through the snow, and then he broke a window and climbed in."

"Obviously not a career criminal," I said, snorting.

"Yeah, the guy was about as sneaky as a rhinoceros." Officer Beadle chuckled. "Plus the door was unlocked. He could've just walked right in."

"Was it Mitch Van Den Berg?"

"I can't comment on that, hon."

He took another sip from his thermos, then thoughtfully pulled a foam cup out of a sack and poured some coffee for me, too. Officer Beadle, in particular, sort of thinks of me as an honorary member of the force. I do more detective work around town than any of them, after all.

"Did he get away with anything?" I asked, taking a very small sip. I'm not much for coffee, but it was cold outside, and the coffee was hot. And investigators always drink coffee when they're discussing cases outside. There's a scene showing that in practically every cop movie ever made.

"Nope. We caught him rooting through the file cabinets, making a mess. He didn't find anything, though. He was empty-handed when we took him in."

"So he got arrested?" I asked.

Right away, I thought of Jennifer. I had hoped that if he didn't get the list, they wouldn't have to arrest him!

"Yeah," said Officer Beadle. "Murray got to take him into the station to book him and everything, but me? I drew the short straw. So I'm stuck here, putting up the police tape. Is that just my luck or what? First guy to get booked in a month, and I'm missing out on all the action."

"I didn't think he'd get arrested!" I said. "I thought you'd just scare him off!"

"Yeah," said Officer Beadle. "If he'd gone through the door, we probably would have just told him to get lost. But when someone breaks a window and climbs in, you sort of have to arrest them, you know."

I suddenly felt terrible. I'd gotten Jennifer's dad arrested! She was going to be horrified.

I knew how she felt. I was feeling more horrified myself all the time by how messed up things had been. It really, really stinks to find out you were wrong about something you believed in. But just being wrong about the faculty couldn't be as bad as finding out your dad was arrested. I was going to have to make it up to her somehow.

The best thing I could do was figure out who was really responsible for the bee being so messed up and bring them to justice. I'd get some more proof and have them dead to rights.

And I'd show everyone at a time when the whole town couldn't possibly ignore me: right in the middle of the all-school spelling bee.

17
JENNIFER

alibi—noun. Proof offered by persons accused of a crime that they were elsewhere at the time of the crime. *Harlan had the perfect alibi when someone accused him of sticking his finger into the blueberry pie—he couldn't have done it, because at the time of the pie poking he was busy using that finger to pick his nose!*

Okay. One of the things people have said is that I was with Dad when he broke in. Anyway, that's what Marianne is saying. But I wasn't. The police know it—I wasn't with him when they caught him. And I have an alibi, too. Friday was the night of the Shakespeare Club meeting in Cornersville Trace.

Mom drove me, as usual, and spent the entire trip drilling me on my spelling—I didn't miss a single word, so I didn't get any particularly bad lectures.

"Now," Mom said, when we pulled up to the bookstore, "you ask the people there whether it's true that there were no spelling rules in Shakespeare's day. I still think that Mrs. Jonson is just trying to sabotage you."

"I'll ask, Mom," I said. "Bye!" And I ran out of the car like I was running away from a herd of angry elephants with machine guns, across the parking lot and into the store.

I love the Shakespeare Club. No one is just there to put it on their college application. In fact, most of the people there are way too old to be worried about grades or colleges or résumés—they're just there because they like Shakespeare. Nobody joins the Just Say No Club because they enjoy talking about the dangers of drug abuse.

When I walked into the bookstore, I felt like a whole different person. Like the person I wanted to be. Partly because a lot of the older people there think it's pretty fascinating that someone my age would want to join, and they're all really nice to me. No one ever, ever tells me anything about what a great speller Val was when I'm there, and I know that they'd still like me even if I came in dead last at the bee.

"Hi, Jennifer!" said Warren, one of the older guys who usually came to the meeting.

"Hi!" I said. Then David, Peter, and Greg, all of whom were older than my parents, waved and said hello to me.

They were having a rowdy argument, as usual. Believe it or not, there were times when the place was more like a wrestling match than a book club. This time, David was saying it was a well-established fact that the witch scenes in *Macbeth* were written by a guy named Thomas Middleton.

Most of the people agreed—David explained to me that

writers in those days stole from each other all the time, including Shakespeare—but Horatio was furious at the very notion. He was calling David an "addlepated simpleton," and I was afraid he was going to throw a chair at someone any minute. Horatio believes that Shakespeare didn't write *anything*, and claims to have some sort of proof that it was really written by some guy who was a member of the Brickcutters.

Horatio is nuts, of course. But he starts some really super fights. And whether Shakespeare was really a writer (which he totally was) strikes me as a much better reason to get in a fight than whether to put a bee on a spelling bee poster.

I bought a muffin from the little café and sat down with my copy of *Titus Andronicus*, right next to a woman named Carol. She used to teach Shakespeare courses at the college in the city before she retired.

"Hi, Carol!" I said.

"Jennifer!" she said. "It's always good to see you."

People at most activities do not say "It's always good to see you." They usually greet you by saying "Let's get to work, people!"

Remember how I was talking earlier about the person I want to be? Carol is a lot like that person—she even calls herself an "old hippie" sometimes. She knows *everything*. She lives in a tiny apartment in the city, even though I think she could afford a big house if she wanted one. She never wears socks, for some reason. And when I told her I hate going to activities just to pad my college application, she said, "So you want an education, not just a bunch of headlines to staple to your chest?" See? She totally gets it.

"I have a question," I said to her. "Is it true that there weren't really any spelling rules in Shakespeare's day?"

"Sort of," she said. "People sort of *knew* that there was a right and wrong way to spell things, but no one could really agree on what they were, and most people didn't really care. They just figured that as long as people knew what they meant, it was good enough. Most people couldn't read, anyway."

So it was true. Mrs. Jonson wasn't just trying to psych me out. That would mean that they didn't have bees back then at all.

Come to think of it, I wonder how spelling bees got started. I mean, some guy must have said "You know what might be fun? Let's get a bunch of people together and have them stand around spelling stuff!" What a nut that guy must have been.

"Well, enough about spelling," I said. "Let's talk about Shakespeare!"

I told her all about the stuff I'd been reading in the past week, and she cleared up a lot of the stuff I was confused about. Then we started in on the regular group discussion. It was like school, only *so* much better. The person leading the discussion didn't have to tell anyone to stop chewing gum or take off their hat, even though some people *were* chewing gum and wearing hats. And when someone said a curse word, all the group leader did was cough and nod his head over in my direction, like he was saying "Hey! Kid in the room!" There was no threat of detention, no threat of being made to miss recess.

Sometimes things went over my head, but I didn't mind.

In fact, I liked it. It showed that they weren't dumbing things down for me. And it didn't matter if I wasn't able to follow everything, because there wasn't going to be a test or anything. I'd never get an extra picture in the yearbook or any extra credit for being there. I'd just be smarter.

Naturally, before the meeting was even over, my mother showed up to ruin it for me.

"Jennifer!" she shouted, using her outside voice indoors. "We have to leave."

"Mom!" I said. "We still have half an hour left!"

"I know," she said, looking really upset. "But we're leaving. Come on, Jennifer."

I sighed, rolled my eyes, and picked up my book.

Everyone there said "Good-bye," even Horatio. I started to say it back, but my mother grabbed my wrist and started to drag me right out to the parking lot, like I was a five-year-old or something. I'll bet hippies never drag their kids like that.

"What did I do?" I asked.

"Nothing," she said. "Not that I know of, anyway. It's your father."

"What's wrong?" I had gotten so wrapped up in talking about Shakespeare that I'd actually forgotten what he was doing that night.

"He was caught breaking into the school. We have to go bail him out of jail."

18
MUTUAL

origami—noun. The Japanese art of paper folding. *Jason had to learn to do all sorts of origami tricks so that when he was caught folding his paper into an origami Bowie knife, he could make it look as though he were making an origami swan.*

Since I did not leave the house the whole weekend, and we did not regularly receive newspapers, I did not know what had happened at Gordon Liddy Community School on Friday evening until Monday. I spent most of my weekend immersed in spelling, listening to the music of Paranormal Execution, and considering a career in the field of eating things for money. I had seen Jake Wells doing so in the cafeteria, and felt that it might be an excellent career for me, as well, if I ever got tired of being a spelling hustler.

So nothing prepared me for the scene I encountered when I arrived on Monday morning—the classroom was total chaos. People were shouting at each other and throwing things around.

Marianne Cleaver was pointing her finger at Jennifer Van Den Berg, shouting that she was a cheater.

Jennifer was sitting at her desk with her head down, looking as though she was crying. She was covering her ears with her hands and had curled her knees up onto her chest as Marianne shouted at her.

Tony Ostanek was standing on his desk, pointing at Amber Hexam and calling her a witch. Amber was responding by going cross-eyed and chanting something at Tony.

Jason, meanwhile, appeared to be coming to her defense by folding a sheet of paper into a four-pointed ninja star, which, he had told me, was the deadliest origami weapon known to man.

It was a riot!

This was what I had been expecting on my first day!

"What is going on?" I asked out loud.

Jake walked over to me. "Didn't you hear?" he asked.

"No," I said.

He pulled a newspaper out of his backpack and showed it to me.

It was dated Saturday morning.

BREAK-IN AT GORDON LIDDY

DID PRINCIPAL FLOREN KNOW?

PRESTON—Acting on an anonymous tip, authorities apprehended Mitchell Van Den Berg breaking into Gordon Liddy Community School on Friday night. Van Den Berg, whose daughter Jennifer is considered a strong contender at this year's all-school spelling bee, now less than a week away, is believed to have been seeking the school's master word list.

Dressed all in black, Van Den Berg was caught in the office at approximately 8 p.m., rooting through a file cabinet, having gained entrance to the school through a window he had broken. Apparently he did not realize that the front door of the school was actually unlocked.

"Beats me why he broke the darned window," said Police Officer Jim Beadle, who teaches children about the dangers of drug abuse as the leader of the school's Just Say No Club. "If he had just shown up dressed as a plumber or something and walked through the front door, I wouldn't have even pursued him. But when I saw a guy dressed like a burglar breaking a window, I obviously had to act."

In a statement released hours later, Van Den Berg accused the school of having already supplied the word list to Marianne Cleaver, another top contender, and alleged that Jason "Skeleton" Keyes and Mutual Scrivener, a new student, had also acquired the master word list. Cleaver's parents vehemently denied the accusation, as did Keyes's. Scrivener's parents could not be reached for comment.

Cleaver's parents, in fact, suggested that Principal Floren may have known of or even authorized the break-in, which would explain why the door had been left unlocked, and how Van Den Berg had been able to access the filing cabinet in the first place.

Principal Floren has denied all charges, stating that he did not think to lock the door because locking up is normally the duty of Mrs. Rosemary, his secretary, who left earlier than he did Friday. Given the lack of evidence against him, the Preston police do not currently consider Principal Floren to be a suspect.

Van Den Berg was released on $500 bail, and has been charged with breaking, entering, and damaging school property. Since the word list he sought was not obtained, his daughter will still be allowed to enter the all-school bee. Officer Beadle describes her as a member in good standing of the Just Say No Club.

```
      The master word list, however, re-
   mains missing.
```

As I was finishing the article, Jason finished his paper ninja star and threw it at Tony to protect Amber. It missed him and landed on Jake's desk.

Just then, Mrs. Boffin arrived in the room.

"Good morning, class," said Mrs. Boffin. This time, though, nobody said anything in response. Even Marianne was still too busy shouting at Jennifer, who had not looked up.

Mrs. Boffin began banging on her desk with a ruler until everyone finally quieted down. "I said, 'Good morning, class!'" she said, a little more loudly than before.

"Good morning, Mrs. Boffin," I said, along with Marianne.

"I will hear no more of this shouting!" shouted Mrs. Boffin. "No one in this class had anything to do with the unpleasant activities of Friday evening, and other than the broken window, no harm was done."

"Then what happened to the master word list?" asked Marianne. "It was missing from the school!"

"That will be enough, Marianne," said Mrs. Boffin. "There is to be no more shouting, no more fighting, and no more accusations of cheating or sabotage."

Everything calmed down for a moment, until she looked over at Jake Wells.

"Jake," she asked, "what's that on your desk?"

"I don't know, Mrs. Boffin," he said, looking down at it.

Mrs. Boffin walked over to him. "A four-pointed ninja

star!" she said, looking down at the star Jason had thrown. "Don't you realize that this is in flagrant violation of our zero-tolerance weapons policy?"

"I didn't make it, Mrs. Boffin!" said Jake.

"Then what is it doing on your desk?" she asked. "Jake, you are to report to the office at once!"

"But I didn't make it!" Jake shouted.

"Then who did?" she asked.

"I did it," said Jason, standing up. "I made the ninja star. Tony Ostanek was threatening Amber, so I threw it at him, and it landed on Jake's desk."

"Amber's a witch!" Tony shouted out. "And probably Marianne, too!"

"No!" shouted Harlan. "Marianne's not a witch, she's a robot!" Harlan almost seemed to be enjoying the scene.

"Enough!" shouted Mrs. Boffin. "Jason, gather your things and go to the office at once! The rest of you, stay in your seats. We did not come here to fight today. We did not come here to accuse each other of cheating, sabotage, or witchcraft. We came to discuss Vasco da Gama, the first explorer to sail around the southern tip of Africa and go all the way to India, and that's exactly what we're going to do!"

Jason gathered up his backpack and bravely began walking toward the door.

Amber was starting to cry. "I'll wait for you, Jason!" she shouted.

He turned back, winked at her, and walked out the door. I believe that was the first romantic act I had ever witnessed in my life.

Gunther opened his mouth, as though he was about to

make fun of them, but Harlan shushed him. Even he, as class clown, understood the gravity of what we had just witnessed. It was not an event to be laughed at.

"Jake," said Mrs. Boffin. "You still have to go to the office, too."

"But I didn't make the star!" he said.

"It was on your desk," she said sternly. "And possession is nine-tenths of the law. I will leave your fate in the hands of the office. Go."

Looking like he was about to cry, Jake stood up and picked up his backpack.

As he stepped away from his desk, Harlan began to clap for him, shouting, "Go get 'em, Jake! We know you didn't do it!" Then Tony joined in, followed by Chrissie. Soon half of the class was applauding Jake as though he had just eaten a turnip covered in pickle juice, hot sauce, and the strange substance that the cafeteria called Santa Fe dressing.

"Enough!" Mrs. Boffin said, as Jake disappeared into the hallway.

"That isn't fair, Mrs. Boffin!" shouted Chrissie.

"These are the rules, Chrissie," said Mrs. Boffin.

"But it isn't fair!" she said. "What's going to happen to them?"

"That will be up to Principal Floren," said Mrs. Boffin. "And questioning his conduct is against the rules for students, too, Chrissie. So I suggest you just maintain faith that the system works and forget about it! Now, let us begin discussing Vasco da Gama!"

It took a moment for me to digest all that I had just seen. Jason had just broken a school rule to protect Amber, and

123

then offered himself up for possible expulsion to keep Jake out of trouble. Even though he had failed to clear Jake's name, it had been a very noble thing to try. He always told me that he was corrupt, but now I was not sure that he was corrupt at all.

Amber sat in the desk next to mine, quietly saying, "He's so brave!" over and over.

As Mrs. Boffin spoke about the explorers, I felt as though I were hearing "Hero's Journey," one of my favorite Paranormal Execution songs, playing in my head, but it had nothing to do with the voyage of Vasco da Gama.

19
CHRISSIE

Excerpt from notebook #32:
Jake has ended up in trouble for things that were not
his fault ~~10 11 12~~ 13 times. . . .

Detectives aren't supposed to get their emotions involved in a case. But you can't always help it when you see the look on a victim's face.

And as long as I live, I'll never forget the look on Jennifer's face Monday morning. She was so red, you'd have thought she must have been really embarrassed—I mean, it was the kind of red you'd think could only be achieved by someone who had just been caught dancing naked in the cafeteria. But her eyes were just as red as her face, which meant that she hadn't just been embarrassed, she'd also been crying.

Right away, I told her how sorry I was—she and I both knew who the anonymous tipster who had told the police that someone was breaking in that night had been. I told her I had never meant for them to arrest him. I thought they'd just catch him on the grounds, and he'd say, "Oh, I was just here to look at the flowers" or something, and leave. Or that he'd see the cops on the premises, chicken out, and leave. I didn't count on him to dress up like a burglar and break a window.

Jennifer said it wasn't my fault, that what I was hoping for was what she had thought would happen, too. She said it was her dad's own fault for breaking the window instead of going through the door like a normal person. But I still felt bad. And as soon as Marianne arrived and started shouting, Jennifer started bawling.

It was Marianne who started the riot in the classroom on Monday morning. It was her shouting that made Tony pick up the cue and start shouting at Amber and calling her a witch. And it was that that made everyone else start shouting at everyone else. Marianne should have been the one suspended. Sure, Jason had thrown the paper star at Tony, but it was only to defend Amber's honor—it wasn't the best idea, but he was only trying to stick up for a girl that he liked. And Jake certainly shouldn't have been in trouble— he hadn't done a thing. And everyone knew it.

They were in serious trouble, too. Neither of them was very good at spelling. That meant that they'd be punished as harshly as Floren could manage.

Something was rotten at Gordon Liddy Community School. I still hadn't figured everything out, but Principal Floren was certainly cheating at the bee by giving Mutual the word list, and I was still guessing that it was Mrs. Boffin who was behind the break-in. I just didn't have the proof yet.

But one thing I did know was that I had to act. As far as I was concerned, if the school was messing with one of us, they were messing with all of us. If keeping the students from cheating and sabotaging each other was my job, then it was also my job to protect students from injustice. I understood that now.

This wasn't about my quest to know everything about everyone anymore. It wasn't about upholding law and order in exchange for extra cookies and a permanent hall pass. It wasn't about stupid and pointless rules that didn't make sense and did more harm than good. This was about truth, justice, and democracy. Three things that didn't exist at Gordon Liddy Community School. Not anymore.

There was a time, not long before, when I would have been glad that Jason and Jake were in trouble. I would have tried to get other people in trouble, too. But now I knew better.

An hour went by, and Jason and Jake still hadn't come back from the office. I hated to think what might be happening to them, and I decided it was all up to me to make things right—even if it cost me everything else I had worked for. I owed it to them. I'd gotten them in trouble plenty of times before. It was time I started my work protecting them from the school.

While Mrs. Boffin was writing about Vasco da Gama on the marker board with her back turned on the rest of the class, I moved over to Jason's desk, then asked Amber to switch spots with me so I could sit right next to Mutual. She agreed. When she sat down, she started pulling things out of Jason's desk and holding them up to her chest.

Boffin kept writing, and I leaned over to Mutual.

"Do you have that list Floren gave you?" I asked.

"How do you know about that?" he whispered, with his eyes as wide as a couple of dinner plates behind his glasses.

"I know everything that goes on here," I said. "What was on the list?"

"I am not supposed to talk about it," he said.

"It's all right," I said, flashing my permanent hall pass. "Floren trusts me with these things. I'm sort of in charge of keeping order around here. Can you show me the list?"

He looked at the hall pass for a second, then said, "Well, okay. But I do not have it with me. I have hardly looked at it."

"Can you bring it tomorrow?" I asked.

He nodded. I would have liked to have had it in my possession to wave in Floren's face, but I'd just have to get Jake and Jason out of trouble without it.

I flashed my pass at Mrs. Boffin and marched out of the room into the office. Jake and Jason were sitting in chairs against the wall. Jake had clearly been crying. Jason was trying really hard to look like he hadn't.

"Chrissie!" Mrs. Rosemary said when she saw me. "I figured we'd be hearing from you today. Do you have any information?"

"I need to speak to Principal Floren immediately," I said.

"Go right in," she told me.

I walked past, giving Jason and Jake a nod and a wink as I passed them.

Inside his office, Floren looked like he hadn't slept all weekend.

"Oh, thank goodness you're here," he said. "We're in a

regular mess over this whole break-in. I'm sure you have some information that we can use, right?"

"Not that you can use," I said. "I'm here to bargain for the release of Jason Keyes and Jake Wells."

"I'm afraid that can't be done," said Floren. "The media has been hounding me all weekend. People are saying I had something to do with the break-in. Or that I can't keep control of what goes on here. They're saying I can't keep the students safe! Do you realize what that means?"

"It means they don't know the half of it," I said calmly.

"No! It means my job is in serious trouble!" he said. "I have to show that the safety of the students is one of my top priorities! Even suspicion of the use of a weapon cannot be allowed, and that includes a paper ninja star. It's unfortunate, but I had to make an example out of them. People are starting to say I'm not a good enough principal. If I want to look like a winner, I have to beat somebody. And I'm beating the troublemakers. That makes me a peacemaker."

"What's going to happen to them?" I asked.

"Well, since he isn't known to have thrown the star, Jake will probably just be suspended for two weeks," said Floren. "Jason, however, is facing expulsion. If he pleads guilty, he might just be suspended for the rest of the year, but it's in the hands of the school board."

I stared at him, and he stared at me. It was like in one of those cop movies where the good-guy cop has to confront the sheriff that he knows is taking bribes from the bad guys. Except that the sheriffs in those movies always sound like they're from Texas, and I'm pretty sure Principal Floren was born here in Preston.

"I think," I said, "that it's in your best interest to issue a pardon."

"What are you talking about?" he said.

"I've seen the surveillance footage," I said. "I know you gave Mutual a word list. And if you don't want the whole town to know about it, you'll issue a pardon to both of them."

"Chrissie!" he said. "How did you get that disc?"

"Never mind," I said.

"I should have guessed. You're the one who has the master word list, aren't you?"

"My object in taking it was merely to prevent Mr. Van Den Berg from taking the list. I had to do something when you didn't respond to the tip I gave you about him breaking in."

"I don't understand this," he said. "We've always trusted you. And now you're blackmailing me?"

I had never, ever used any of my data to blackmail anyone before. But things were different now. Gordon Liddy had gone berserk.

"Don't act like you're the one that's been betrayed!" I said. "My job was to uphold law and order and make sure the spelling bee was a fair contest. And it turns out that there was no law or order to uphold. Now, do we have a deal, or don't we?"

He sat for a second, looking over at the portrait of Abraham Lincoln that hung on the wall. "Deal," he said, finally.

"That's not all," I said. "Besides the pardon, I want you to guarantee me the seat behind the sound equipment at the spelling bee."

"Why?" he asked.

"I have my reasons," I said, thinking of Harlan's quest to belch on the microphone. I hadn't decided to help him for sure yet, but this was my last chance to be prepared. "That's the deal. I get the soundboard seat, Jason and Jake go free, and I don't turn the disc of you giving Mutual the list over to the newspapers today."

He sat staring for a second. I tried not to smirk.

"It's a deal," he said. "But all of the privileges we've granted you are hereby revoked, including your permanent hall pass."

"It's all meaningless now, anyway," I said. "I'll expect Jason and Jake back in class within five minutes."

And I dropped my pass on his desk and walked out the door.

I didn't work for the school anymore.

I worked for the students.

20

INTEROFFICE MEMO
FROM: Principal Floren
TO: Mrs. Boffin
CC: Mrs. Rosemary

In light of the fact that paper is not currently considered a weapon, Jake Wells and Jason Keyes are hereby granted a full pardon by executive order of Richard M. Floren, Principal.

INTEROFFICE MEMO
FROM: Principal Floren
TO: All staff

Please note that by executive order, Chrissie Woodward's permanent hall pass has been revoked, along with all extra privileges she has heretofore been granted. Since her services are no longer being utilized, it will be up to all of us to keep an eye on Harlan Sturr, Jason Keyes, and any other student suspected of planning to cheat at the spelling bee on Friday. The police have turned down my request to station three officers around the school at all times.

INTEROFFICE MEMO
FROM: Mrs. Rosemary
TO: Principal Floren

The assault was with a four-pointed ninja star, the deadliest of origami weapons, not with a sheet of paper. Are you sure that the pardon is wise?

INTEROFFICE MEMO
FROM: Principal Floren
TO: Mrs. Rosemary

While four-pointed ninja stars are certainly deadly, we have no proof that it was used in an assault, and they are not currently listed as weapons. I am taking steps to close this loophole. In the meantime, my authority as principal grants me the power to issue pardons such as these. I have determined that neither Wells nor Keyes poses an actual threat to the other students or to the spelling bee. The best thing is to put the matter behind us.

INTEROFFICE MEMO
FROM: Principal Floren
TO: All staff

Two students involved in an attempted assault with a four-pointed paper ninja star escaped punishment today due to a loophole in school policy. I have drafted a request to the school board recommending changes that will close the loophole.

Should my proposal be granted, sheets of hard-cornered notebook paper, which can be folded into the deadly weapons in question, will be considered contraband under our zero-tolerance weapons policy. Only rounded-edge paper, which is more difficult to craft into a deadly weapon, will be permitted, and the only allowable type of paper will be construction paper, which is less likely to give students a paper cut. Keeping our students safe must be our top priority.

INTEROFFICE MEMO
FROM: Mrs. Boffin
TO: Mrs. Rosemary
First of all, why did he think they could position three police officers around the school at all times? There are only three police officers on the local squad to begin with! Second of all, do they even make rounded-corner construction paper? Has he gone mad?

INTEROFFICE MEMO
FROM: Mrs. Rosemary
TO: Mrs. Boffin
Of course they make rounded-cornered construction paper. Richard M. Floren's authority as principal is total, and he remains the leader of our school. I advise you not to question his

sanity. The fiasco this weekend has him under untold stress, after all.

INTEROFFICE MEMO
FROM: Frank Ruggles, Janitor
TO: All staff

I need to encourage all staff to be vigilant in a crackdown against spitting on campus. Since Friday evening, there has apparently been a rash of spitting in the hallways and on the grounds. Cleaning up these "loogeys," as the students call them, is preventing me from performing my usual custodial duties. Any student seen spitting in the hallways should be sent to the office at once. Please inform your students that this will not be tolerated.

INTEROFFICE MEMO
FROM: Principal Floren
TO: All staff

Just a reminder that, especially in these troubled days, no visitor is allowed on school grounds without a permit. No exceptions are to be made, not even for little old ladies. If you see any visitor without a visible guest pass, including old ladies, please attempt to apprehend them and call the police. Security will be especially tight on Friday for the spelling bee—all visitors and members of the press will be required to display their passes at all times. No exceptions!

INTEROFFICE MEMO
FROM: Mrs. Rosemary
TO: All staff

Wonderful news! I have just received a call from Agnes Milhous of the Burger Baron. She and the co-owner, Helen Bernowski, have offered to cater the spelling bee free of charge. Each staff member is to receive a free lunch on Friday, along with each contestant!

21
JENNIFER

omphaloskepsis—noun. The act of contemplating one's navel. *If they had omphalo-skepsis competitions, Marianne would make it her business to become the champion.*

When I left for school on Monday, it was the first time I'd been out of my bedroom since we'd bailed Dad out. Mom and Dad hadn't been able to get me to come downstairs. I didn't want to talk to either of them just then, and I sure as heck didn't want to go to any activities. So I stayed in my room, eating the sandwiches I let them bring in, reading Shakespeare and imagining I lived far, far away. Someplace that wasn't as depressing and lonely as Preston. Some nice woods full of hippies playing guitars and singing about rainbows where I could hang out during the day, and a little apartment in the city above a theater where I could hear the show every night if I put my ear to the floor.

The Shakespeare play I studied most over the weekend was *Richard III*, a play about an ugly duke who lies, cheats, and murders his way into being king. He reminded me a lot of my dad right about then. Only at least the duke was going for something big, like being a king. My dad was just trying to cheat his way into getting his daughter an unfair advantage in a school spelling bee.

Mom tried to talk to me a little bit through the door, but I told her to go away. She was probably just trying to get me to come out and go to the recycling club, anyway.

I finally got out of my room to go downstairs on Monday morning before school. Mom gave me a big cup of hot chocolate, which made up things a bit on her end. Hot chocolate doesn't solve all of life's problems, but I'd say it comes pretty close.

Dad was on the phone, screaming to someone that he'd been framed, and that I was the only one NOT cheating. Then he yelled that I was going to take first place anyway.

I spent most of Monday morning at school with my head down on my desk—I knew Marianne was shouting horrible things at me, but I tried to just tune her out. I was used to tuning the rest of the world out, of course, and I was pretty good at it, but this really put me to the test.

At first I tried to put every bit of my energy into staring at my belly button, but that didn't work for long, so I ended up spending most of the morning distracting myself by trying to remember all of the opening speech from *Richard III*. That worked pretty well.

I wasn't able to shut myself off enough not to notice what was going on with Jason and Jake, though.

After they were sent away, there was this energy in the class that I think everyone must have been able to feel.

We'd all been in class together for so many years that it was almost like we were a family. Even though we had been fighting a lot that morning, when something like that happened, it was like it happened to all of us. I really think that if Jason and Jake hadn't been back in class before lunch, there would have been some sort of rebellion or something. Like we all would have stormed the office and taken over the school. I would have been proud to join in.

But after Jason and Jake were pardoned and let back into class, things calmed down quite a bit. I was able to enjoy my food at lunch—after a weekend of living on bologna sandwiches, even the three-bean casserole from the hot lunch tasted pretty good, and that's saying something. Normally the stuff tastes like shampoo. Jake sat next to me, wolfing it down with gusto.

"I'm glad they let you go," I said to him.

"Me too!" he said. "Sorry about what happened to your dad. Everyone knows you had nothing to do with it. Everyone but her, anyway." He motioned his head at Marianne, who had brought her dictionary to lunch with her.

"It's all right." I sighed. "I'm glad he didn't get the word list, at least. I wouldn't want to have it."

"I just hope you really clobber Marianne on Friday," Jake said. "You know, she has never once given me a dollar to eat anything."

I made it through the rest of the day feeling a lot better, and that night at home, I even went downstairs. I was still trying to avoid Dad, but I figured that at least getting arrested would probably calm him down a little.

Naturally, I was wrong.

I was just finishing dinner when there was a knock at the door. I went to open it, and found James and Darlene Cleaver, Marianne's parents, standing on the porch.

"Jennifer," said Mr. Cleaver. He gave me a dirty look, and I gave him one back. I mean, it was my DAD who had broken in—not me. Looking at ME like that was uncalled for.

"We'd like to come in, please," said Mrs. Cleaver.

"I'm sorry," I said. "I'm not supposed to let strangers in."

"We're not strangers," said Mrs. Cleaver. "We're Marianne's parents. Step aside, please."

And with that, they walked right past me into the house.

"Wait!" I shouted, following them toward the kitchen, where my parents were sitting. I was pretty sure that they were breaking the law by just charging in like that.

"James!" my father shouted, standing up as though he was ready for a fistfight.

"Mitchell!" said Mr. Cleaver.

"What's the meaning of this?" asked my father. "Charging onto my property without permission? You're trespassing!"

"That's funny coming from you," said Mr. Cleaver. "Imagine! Mitchell Van Den Berg, telling people not to break into a place!"

"I'm warning you, James," said Dad. "I know kung fu!"

"Let's just make this quick," said Mr. Cleaver. "We want Jennifer out of the bee."

"Never!" Mom shouted. "You'll have to kill us first!"

"No!" I shouted. "Nobody has to kill anybody!"

"Jennifer, stay out of this!" my father shouted. "This doesn't concern you."

"Yes it does!" I shouted. "It's all ABOUT me!"

But no one listened. Why should they? I was just a new kind of cola to be marketed to colleges. No one cares what cola thinks.

"Enough!" said Dad. "You have a lot of nerve, Cleaver! You don't see us asking you to pull Marianne out, even though everyone knows she has the master word list!"

"Lies!" shouted Mr. Cleaver. "You just can't handle the fact that our Marianne is a genius!"

"Genius shmenius!" shouted Mom. "I'll bet they put her in remedial math in high school!"

Mrs. Cleaver screamed and lunged at Mom, grabbing for her hair. Dad jumped forward and grabbed Mr. Cleaver by the suspenders.

"Stop!" I shouted. "Everyone stop!" I grabbed the nearest frying pan and spoon I could find and started banging away.

Everyone paused in their tracks for just a second and turned to look at me.

"Can't we work this out without fighting?" I asked.

They paused for one more second, then went back to fighting.

I ran up to my room to hide. Ten minutes later the shouting stopped, and I heard the Cleavers' car driving away.

"Jennifer!" Dad shouted. "Come down here, please."

I stepped back out of my room and wandered downstairs. The kitchen looked as though a tornado had come through it. The cookware was all over the floor. The kitchen table was overturned. There was a lot of broken glass in evidence. I really, really hoped that no one had slashed anyone with a broken bottle. There was no blood around, at least. I guess Dad didn't use all of the combat training he's always bragging about having gotten in military school. Or maybe they did about as good a job teaching him to fight as they did teaching him to sneak into buildings.

"What happened?" I asked. "Who won the fight?"

"We did," he said proudly. "They ran out after just a couple of minutes."

"They didn't really get hurt, did they?" I asked.

"No," he said. "No one was hurt. But when someone breaks into your house, you have a right to defend your family. And your daughter's right to be in the spelling bee. Get your coat. We're going to get the last word!"

"Please," I said. "I don't want to get involved in this stuff."

"Jennifer," he said, "when you get into the corporate world, you'll find out that a lot of times you have to do things that you don't want to do. Now get your coat!"

I grabbed my coat and followed him out into the car, trying to sulk as visibly as possible. I wanted to make it clear that I was going under protest. I scowled so hard it hurt.

"Where are we going?" I asked, not sure that I wanted to know.

"You'll see," he said.

We drove through the streets of Preston, and I noticed that a handful of houses—the ones where my friends lived—had yard signs sticking out of the snow. Things that

142

said stuff like "Go Get 'Em, Tony," and "Gunther is a W-I-N-N-E-R!" The light-up message-board sign outside the appliance store said "Good luck, spellers." So did the one outside the church. Everywhere I looked, there was something about the spelling bee. Another reminder.

We drove past the school and over into Marianne's neighborhood.

"I want you to see how we Van Den Bergs stand up for ourselves," Dad said.

"Please tell me we're not going to break into her house," I said.

"No," he said. "But we're going to make sure she has an awfully hard time studying that word list of hers!"

We pulled up right in front of her house, and Dad told me to roll down the windows. As I did, he turned on the radio, tuned it in to a rock station, and turned the volume up as high as it would go.

"Let's see how well she can concentrate now!" he shouted gleefully. "This is what the army does to get terrorists to come out of bunkers!"

I buried my face in my hands. Obviously I wouldn't be able to concentrate, either. Sitting right by the speakers hurt my ears a lot more than it would hurt Marianne's, and at least she had her windows shut.

I was pretty sure they didn't live nearby, but what if Mutual and his family had driven by right then? Mutual wouldn't want anything to do with me. And I wouldn't blame him. That evening, I didn't feel like I was weird. I felt like I was nuts.

After a few seconds, Marianne appeared at the window,

scowling down and shouting something at me, though I couldn't make out what it was. Her parents came outside and tried to run my dad off, but he'd just drive a few feet out of the way when they approached the car. This, I gathered, could take a while. My dad laughed like a maniac and shouted that I was the Queen of Spelling. I'd never been so embarrassed in all my life.

We were out there for about ten minutes before my dad saw the Cleavers making a phone call. He worried that they were calling the police, and took off, since getting caught waging war on another speller wouldn't help him much when he went to court.

"See that?" he said to me as he drove away. "*That's* how we Van Den Bergs stand up for ourselves. We don't let anybody push us around!"

It was starting to snow again—for the first time in a few weeks. The cold wind and snowflakes blew into the open window and stung my cheeks. But this time I didn't enjoy it.

I didn't hate Marianne, exactly. Heck, I even wished she would join the synchronized swimming team, the one club that she had never joined. I can't tell you how stupid I feel doing routines by myself at the meets.

When we got home, I tried to call her.

"What do you want?" she asked. I didn't blame her for sounding mad.

"I want to apologize," I said. "I think this whole fight is stupid, and I'm SO sorry that my dad tried to bug you tonight."

"Ha!" she said. "You're going down, Van Den Berg. I don't care about the fight, either, because I WANT you in the bee. I want the satisfaction of beating you into the ground! You're going to get stuck going to some no-name junior college, majoring in liberal arts!"

And she hung up the phone.

I didn't tell her that I really DID plan to major in liberal arts. I know that doesn't usually lead to a job as a CEO, but I don't WANT a job as a CEO! If that was the future Marianne wanted, she could have it, as far as I was concerned.

A second later, it rang again, and I picked it up, hoping it would be Marianne, so I could try to apologize again. But it wasn't. It was Chrissie.

"Hey," she said. "You got a minute?"

"I guess," I said.

"Do you have any clue who it might have been that called your dad the night before the break-in?"

"No," I said. "No idea. Mom and Dad won't tell me. They told me he didn't bribe anyone, though. Whoever it was just wants me to win, too, for some reason."

"Do you think, by any chance, that it might have been Mrs. Boffin?" she asked. "I think there's a chance she might really want you to win the bee."

"What?" I asked. "You think *Boffin* is cheating?"

"Maybe," she said. "Boffin and Floren never liked each other very much, you know. You should see some of the interoffice memos Boffin sends to Mrs. Rosemary. She thinks Floren is off his rocker."

"Wow," I said. "But what does that have to do with the spelling bee?"

"Everything!" said Chrissie. "Ever since Mutual showed

up. If you beat him, Mrs. Boffin can say 'My students beat out the spelling wizard.' And Floren wants Mutual to win so she'll look bad!"

"Wait . . . Floren wants Mutual to win?" I asked. "How do you know?"

"I can't tell. Not yet. But if you think of ANYTHING to do with that phone call, let me know."

"Actually," I said, "there's one thing I forgot. The only thing I actually overheard Dad say that night."

"What was it?" asked Chrissie.

"He said, 'Thank you, sir,' right before he hung up," I said. "There's no way it was Mrs. Boffin. She's not a sir."

"I don't know," said Chrissie. "Maybe he just called her sir to throw you off the trail."

"Come on, Chrissie," I said. "The guy broke into an unlocked building dressed as a burglar! There's no way he'd think to do anything *that* sneaky."

"True," said Chrissie. "I guess I'm back to the drawing board."

I hung up the phone and got into bed. Four more days to go till it was all over.

I would have really liked to just resign from the bee. I'd have to accept the fact that I wouldn't be getting out of any activities, but at least the whole thing would be behind me.

And anyway, I remember what happened to Val. Mom and Dad worked her to the BONE for districts—and for nationals her sixth-grade year, when she won districts, too. She gave up her whole life for spelling—and even Marianne wasn't going as nuts as Val was going by the end of it. And I didn't want that to happen to me. Ever.

But I did want to win. For one thing, I thought I could get Mutual's attention. He hadn't said a word to me since his first day. More than that, though, I really wanted to beat Marianne. I didn't want to wage war on her, but I knew that if I lost, she'd never let me hear the end of it.

Plus I could just hear my dad's voice if I lost. "I broke into a building and blasted rock music at someone's house for you, and you don't win!" he'd say. And next thing I knew, I'd be wearing a uniform and marching all the time.

Why do I have to have a nut for a parent? He's my dad, and I still love him, but sometimes it doesn't seem fair that you get stuck having to love complete maniacs.

I have no problem admitting that I cried myself to sleep that night.

22
MUTUAL

cerebral atrophy—noun. A condition in which the brain becomes weak from too much intense focus and/or concentration. *When told that the best word for the condition of her brain was "cerebral atrophy," Marianne said, "That's T-W-O words!"*

Every day in class that week, almost every student was immersed in a dictionary, working on spelling. Some students quizzed each other on the spelling of various words. And others, I was sure, were still working on sabotage and cheating. Most of them seemed to have been pushed to the very edge of sanity.

The rest of the week was the most exciting time of my life. Finally, the school was starting to seem like I had always imagined public schools to be! The students were rough and rowdy, and corruption was everywhere.

Jason had been hailed as a hero since his return from the office on Monday. I was proud to be his friend. Amber began to hug him regularly, and even kissed him on the cheek occasionally. Almost every time I looked at them, they were holding hands. I continued to study heavy metal, and even came upon the concept of learning an instrument and forming a heavy-metal musical group of my own. After all, Jason had told me that girls loved guys who played in bands, so it would be a sure way to get Jennifer's attention.

Things were not so good between Jennifer and Marianne, though. Both of them had arrived at school on Tuesday looking as though they'd been in a fight, and Jennifer seemed to have a bad cold. By the end of the week, they were being followed around by recess monitors, but I did not understand why at the time.

By Wednesday, Marianne was twitching a lot, and had moved from spelling a word or two in every sentence to spelling almost everything she said. She spelled a lot of words at Jennifer that I certainly hadn't heard before—Jason and Amber assured me that they would not be in the dictionaries my parents bought for me, but they promised to teach them to me.

Every day, Chrissie asked me to bring her the list that Principal Floren had given me, but I kept forgetting it. She was taking more notes than ever, and seemed to be on the verge of a major breakthrough. I was glad to know there was a person like her fighting corruption. After all, she had freed Jason from trouble on Monday. She was a hero, too.

I had, of course, looked at the list Floren had given me by then, but I felt that it was not of much use to me. The words were handwritten and almost impossible to read, and they all appeared to be words I knew, anyway. Despite the policy of helping new students Floren had told me about, I did not require study aids.

Meanwhile, I continued to study the works of Paranormal Execution. Jason gave me more of their recordings, and he taught me how to headbang. Headbanging is a process in which one rapidly moves one's head back and forth in time to rock music. If you are not careful, you can really give yourself a headache. But if you do it right, it is said to be an excellent means by which to relieve stress. I thought that perhaps, if I became an expert, I could teach Jennifer to do it. She seemed very stressed.

After school on Thursday, Mrs. Rosemary met me in the hallway again, and said that Principal Floren would like to see me. I followed her into the office and walked up to Principal Floren's desk—Principal Floren looked almost as stressed as Jennifer had looked at the beginning of the week. His eyes kept darting about the room, as though he thought he was being watched.

"Mutual," he said. "Did you destroy the list?"

"Not yet," I said.

He shuddered, then looked as though he was getting control of himself.

"Now, Mutual," he said. "Tomorrow there is going to be a lot of media present. The bee is going to be on the radio and on public access television and everything. We always broadcast the bee for the parents on the radio, but after the unpleasant events of last week, there will be a lot of extra interest this year. I want you to destroy that list tonight, and be very, very careful not to let any member of the press know that you had ever had that list, all right?"

"All right," I said. "But I do not understand."

"It's very complicated," he said. "I can't tell you too much—it's best, for your own safety, that you be able to deny everything. Let me just tell you this: The school is in danger."

"Danger?" I asked.

"Yes. Danger." he said. "There may be investigations. Inquiries. A lot of people are going to be watching the spelling bee very, very closely. And I need to make sure I can trust you not to tell anyone about that list."

"I will not," I said. I did not mention that I had already told Chrissie.

"Good boy," said Principal Floren. "You may go. And good luck tomorrow."

"Thank you," I said.

I left the building and went to my parents' car, which was parked on the edge of the parking lot.

"Are you all right, Mutual?" asked my mother. "Were there any shootings today?"

"No," I said. "Not today."

"Any rumbles?"

"Not today. There has not been a real rumble since Monday. Since then, there have only been scuffles. And mostly just Marianne trying to scuffle with Jennifer."

"Ha!" said Mother. "Cheaters, the both of them. What did I tell you? The corruption goes all the way to the top in places like this. But you will show them all. Tomorrow, Mutual, is the most important day of your life."

"I know," I said. "I am going to be on television."

23
CHRISSIE

Excerpt from notebook #19:
The broom closet in the front hall is for cleaning supplies. The closet near the gym is mostly cords and cables from gadgets Floren can't figure out how to use.

Those were spelling days, and most kids spelled hard. Spelling practice was taking up most of the afternoon, and even during recess, kids were studying.

By Thursday, the day before Bee Day, tension in the classroom was, by far, the highest I'd ever seen it. Even Tony Ostanek, who normally didn't study for anything, was reading a dictionary all morning. Jason was reading a dictionary, too, when he wasn't being kissed. Amber was doing an awful lot of chants and rituals that seemed to involve kissing Jason's hand or cheek.

Marianne looked like she was doing chants, too, but I knew that she was actually reciting the alphabet, forward and backward, over and over. In between this, she would scowl at Jennifer, or occasionally shout threats at her, demanding that she "surrender." Jennifer had just taken up the strategy of ignoring her altogether. No matter how loudly Marianne shouted her name, Jennifer absolutely would not look up from her copy of *The Complete Works of Shakespeare.*

Harlan was studying hard, too. And I was working harder than ever.

It's weird how things can change in two weeks. Barely a week before, I'd been committed to upholding law and order at the spelling bee. Now I was just as busy, but with a very different plan.

But I was still trying to figure out exactly what was going on. If Boffin wasn't the one who arranged the break-in, why hadn't she given Floren the memo about the break-in that I gave her to give to him? Surely he never saw it, or he would have done something. He wanted Mutual to win, right? Why wouldn't he stop Jennifer's dad from breaking in? Everything was a mystery again.

And, to top it all off, I still didn't know what kind of underwear Mutual wore. It wasn't really important, I know, but it's the little things like that that can really bug you.

In addition to my permanent hall pass, I used to have free access to any closet, shed, or office in the school. I was even allowed into the teachers' lounge on occasion—I was one of only a few kids who had ever been able to see the inside of it. Going back to school on Tuesday, having given all of that up, and becoming just a regular student was a little difficult for me.

I used to have this great belief that the system worked. I was really proud of the work I did. Now I just felt angry. Like I wanted to tear the whole system down, piece by piece, and throw the rubble at the people in charge. And I couldn't think of a better way to start than helping to disrupt the all-school spelling bee.

At lunch, I passed Harlan Sturr a note reading "Recess. Trees. Be alone. XOXO."

Twenty minutes later, at recess, I waited in the wooded area, hiding behind a tree where no one could see me, until he showed up.

"Chrissie?" he called out.

"Here I am," I said, stepping out from my hiding place and, from the looks of things, scaring the crap out of him. "Sorry," I said. "I didn't mean to startle you. But I assume you know why I asked you here."

"Um," he said nervously, "I guess so. But I like you as a friend. That's all."

"I know," I said. "Those 'X's and 'O's were just a cover—that way, if anyone found the note, they'd think I was just here to ask you out. It's safer that way." Rule number one of being a detective: Cover your tracks.

Harlan looked greatly relieved, and I must admit that I was a bit annoyed. Would it have been so terrible if I had wanted to kiss him? I mean, I'm no Brittany Tatomir, but I'm hardly repulsive. And I happen to know that I wear much nicer underwear than she does.

"Anyway," I said, "there's something wrong going on with this bee. I don't know exactly who's involved, but it goes pretty high up."

"Floren?" asked Harlan, his eyes getting wide.

"No comment," I said. "What I'm about to do goes against everything I thought I believed in. But given all the stuff that's going on, there's nothing at the school worth believing in anymore. Belching into the mike makes as much sense as anything else. So I'm going to help you out. Part of my terms with Floren give me the right to sit by the mixing board. When you're about to burp, signal to me by scratching your nose. I'll turn up the sound, and you'll go down in history."

"I . . . I don't know what to say," said Harlan. "Is there anything I can do for you?"

"Just one thing, since you ask," I said. "I have a favor to ask."

"Anything." He leaned in, like he really did expect me to ask him to kiss me or something.

"I need you to see if you can find out what sort of underwear Mutual Scrivener wears."

"What?" asked Harlan, stepping back.

"I already know everything about everyone else," I said. "It's stupid, but it's bothering me that I don't know that about him yet."

"You know what kind of underwear people wear?" he asked. "What kind do I wear?"

"Usually boxers. Funny ones. The kind that have a joke on them or something," I said.

He blushed. "You could have just guessed that," he said.

"None of your briefs are tighty-whities," I went on. "They're mostly dark colors. But you wear boxers about eighty percent of the time."

He blushed again.

"And what else do you know?"

I smirked. "Plenty," I said. "But Mutual wears suspenders *and* a belt *and* a blazer," I said, "which makes it really hard to see anything. With most people, I can just check out their underwear when they bend over, but he's really well covered."

"He doesn't take gym class, either," said Harlan. "So I can't just look over in the locker room. But I'll see what I can do. Okay?"

"Good enough," I said. "It's not like I'm some pervert or anything—I just like to have data about everyone."

"Right," he said. "Say, since you know so much, where's the master word list that disappeared?"

I smiled, unzipped my backpack, and pulled it out.

"Holy crap!" he said. "YOU have it?"

I nodded. "I took it before Jennifer's dad could get his hands on it."

I waited for a second, sure that he was going to ask if he could have it. But he just said, "Awesome," and I put it back in my bag. I really thought he would ask for it, honestly. I thought I knew all about Harlan, but I was starting to find out that there was a lot I didn't know. There's a lot you can find out about someone when you aren't trying to get them in trouble.

I knew all about his underwear, but nothing about his heart.

"Well, make me proud, okay?" I said.

"I will," he said, as solemnly as I'd ever heard him say anything.

He thanked me again and walked off. I stood there in the trees, just watching him, until the end of recess.

After lunch, Marianne and Jennifer were sent to go see Mrs. McGovern, the guidance counselor, who, I supposed, would probably make them use the infamous "I message," a technique for complaining politely, to "resolve their conflict." If that didn't work, she would probably go into her standard speech about whether they wanted to spread "warm fuzzies" or "cold pricklies" around the school—those were her two main techniques.

Neither one of them must have worked, because when they came back, they both had playground monitors following them around, acting as bodyguards. Keeping them away from each other probably would have been my job before; it was kind of gratifying that they needed two people to do it.

At the end of the day, Mrs. Boffin gave us a little speech.

"You have all been attending and competing in spelling bees for six years now," she said. "And tomorrow is the biggest one of your lives. I know a lot of you have worked very hard, but I want to remind you all that the bee is supposed to be fun—it will not be the end of the world if you don't make it to districts. Anyone who is caught cheating will be punished severely. And please, remember not to speak to any member of the press!"

The bell rang a minute later, and we all slowly filed out of the class.

I went to one of my usual hiding places in the bushes and waited until ten minutes had passed. Every day, ten minutes after the bell, Floren would be checking the computer lab to make sure no one had stolen anything, and Mrs. Rosemary would be outside, smoking a cigarette around the back.

I had turned in my hall pass. But I could still get into the office. It wasn't even locked, in fact.

So, as casual as could be, I walked into Floren's office, found the recording labeled "Thursday night"—the night Jennifer's dad got the phone call—and slipped it into my bag. I also took a whole stack of interoffice memos that were sitting on Floren's desk, and a few more from Mrs. Rosemary's.

When I got home and read the memos, I found that one of the memos on Floren's desk was the one about Mr. Van Den Berg breaking in. The one I'd sent him.

That meant that Mrs. Boffin HAD given it to him.

Floren knew about the break-in, all right. He had gotten the memo. He just hadn't told anyone or done anything about it!

Could it be that he didn't want anyone to know about it because he had set it up himself?

It didn't make sense that he'd be helping Jennifer's dad break in, since he was already helping Mutual.

Then again, it seemed like nothing made sense anymore.

24

INTEROFFICE MEMO
FROM: Mrs. Boffin
TO: Mrs. Rosemary

Bee Day is almost here! And not a day too soon—frankly, I'll be very glad to see it come to an end. This morning, Marianne Cleaver asked me to ratify a formal declaration of war against Jennifer Van Den Berg. Jennifer was tuning her out to such an extent that I was afraid she might have snapped, but she seems more upset since Marianne officially "declared war" on her. I hope it won't affect her performance.

INTEROFFICE MEMO
FROM: Mrs. Rosemary
TO: Mrs. McGovern, guidance office

I know that you're very busy with stress counseling and preparing to deal with post-bee trauma counseling next week, but could you squeeze in an appointment for conflict management between Marianne Cleaver and Jennifer Van Den Berg? Marianne is actually trying to formally declare war on Jennifer. Perhaps you could persuade them to give peace a chance.

INTEROFFICE MEMO
FROM: Mrs. McGovern
TO: Mrs. Rosemary
I have space for such an appointment right after the post-lunch recess. Have Mrs. Boffin send them in.

INTEROFFICE MEMO
FROM: Mrs. Rosemary
TO: Mrs. Boffin
I know all about Marianne's attempt to formally declare war on Jennifer—she brought her request into the office and asked us to file it officially. Rather than getting involved, I've arranged for them to attend conflict management with Mrs. McGovern. Please send them both after recess.

INTEROFFICE MEMO
FROM: Mrs. McGovern
TO: Mrs. Rosemary
CC: Mrs. Boffin, Principal Floren
Jennifer is upset, but responding peacefully. However, conflict management has failed to calm Marianne down. As a precautionary measure, I've assigned playground monitors to each to keep them away from each other, and penciled

in post-bee counseling appointments for each of them on Monday.

INTEROFFICE MEMO
FROM: Principal Richard M. Floren
TO: All staff
In light of the disappearance of our master word list, I have arranged for us to use a different list at the bee tomorrow. Instead of our own list, we will use the list from Shaker Heights. Our two schools have historically been rivals, of course, but, as principal, I have opened favorable relations through my friendship with Principal Mao.

INTEROFFICE MEMO
FROM: Principal Richard M. Floren
TO: All staff
As the day draws to a close, please remind your students that they are not to speak with any member of the press prior to the bee!

Let us remember the power of good music to soothe one's jangled nerves. As a means of relieving the students' stress, I have arranged for a pre-bee performance by the Good Times Gang. This should put the students in a much better mood!

25
HARLAN

octogenarian — noun. A person age 80–89. *Walter is not that into sports, other than watching people eat things for dollars, but if they had a show where they had an octogenarian fight with an octopus, he'd watch that.*

Sometimes I think that Chrissie Woodward is a very sick person.

I mean, for one, there's the underwear thing. It's really unnerving to find out that someone else knows what kind of underwear you wear. She's also obsessive. If she knows what one person's favorite food is, she has to know everyone else's favorite food, too.

But that's not to say I don't like her or anything. She got Jake and Jason out of trouble when it looked like Jason could have been expelled. And she was going to help me make history. That's got to count for something. If she wasn't so busy being a very sick person, she could've been a class clown herself. She has the guts for it.

Guts are a useful thing to have, you know. They came in

handy for me on my walk home from school on the day before the bee. Up in front of my house, I saw a couple of old ladies standing around at the end of my driveway.

"Hi, there, Harlan, honey," said one of them.

"Don't call him honey!" shouted the other. "Boys hate that!"

"Uh, hi," I said. My first guess was that they were some sort of obscure relatives of mine. The kind that I'd maybe met once at a wedding when I was five, but didn't remember at all. I figured I should be polite, in case they were about to die and looking for someone to leave all their money to.

"Care to answer some questions about the spelling bee?"

Aha! They were reporters! I knew I wasn't supposed to be talking to the press or anything, but, honestly . . . I just can't resist attention!

"Certainly," I said. "Provided you don't use my name."

"Of course not, dear," said the first old lady.

"Would you say that giving you ten-to-one odds of winning is just about right?" asked the other one. "That a person who gave you chances like that was telling the truth, not trying to cheat a couple of poor, innocent old ladies?"

"Ten to one?" I said. "I'd say I can do a little better than that. I've beaten Jennifer and Marianne in the class bees before!"

"Ah," said the first one. "But you've never beaten Mutual Scrivener. Is it true that he's a genius? Impossible to beat?"

I shrugged. "He seems pretty smart."

"Smarter than Jennifer?" asked the second one.

"Do you suppose it would be worth someone's time to

pull a prank that kept Jennifer from showing up, so Mutual won't have to compete against her?" asked the first. "Because we know how much you love pranks!"

"Shut up, Helen, you ninny!" shouted the second one. "You're supposed to gently hint that, not come right out and ask him! You'll scare him away!"

"Wait a minute," I said. "You want me to keep Jennifer from showing up for the bee?"

They stopped shouting at each other and just stared at me.

"Could you?" asked the first one.

"We'll make it worth your while," added the second one. "You don't have to hurt her, just keep her out of school tomorrow."

"You're the class clown, right?" said the first one. "Maybe you could lock her out of the school and make it look like an accident!"

"No way," I said. "That would be against the code of the class clown."

There's not actually a code of the class clown, exactly. But there sort of is now. I decided there needed to be one after the Rubber Band War to End All Rubber Band Wars got Jake in trouble, so I made one up, and decided to live by it.

Basically, the code is that you should never get other kids in trouble, never cheat, and only pull pranks on people who deserve it. Locking Jennifer out of the school would be WAY against the code. It's also the reason I didn't ask Chrissie for the master word list, even though I'm pretty sure she would have given it to me. I know a lot of rumors go around about me planning to slash people's tires and stuff, but I don't get mixed up in that sort of business—I didn't do that sort of thing even *before* I came up with the code.

"Well, we were just thinking," said the first old lady.

"This interview is over!" I said, starting to walk away. I'd always wanted to say that.

"See, Helen?" shouted the second one. "You scared him off!"

"You're the one who scared him, Agnes!" said the first. "You and that ugly dress you have on!"

They went back to shouting at each other.

"Stop!" I said. "What the heck kind of reporters are you, anyway?"

They stopped shouting again and looked back at me. "We're not reporters," said the first one, who I guessed was called Helen. "We're just interested citizens!"

"That's right," said the other one, Agnes. "Interested harmless old ladies!"

Harmless old ladies who were so interested in the bee that they wanted me to start cheating and sabotaging people!

I guess I should have known right away that they were freaks. But they'd been prepping us for having to deal with a whole bunch of reporters all week, and, anyway, there wasn't anything unusual about having strangers talk to me about the bee. Everywhere I'd been the past couple of weeks—the grocery store, the post office, Hedekker's Appliance Store—people were patting me on the back and wishing me luck. Everyone in town knew the bee was coming up, and everyone was excited about it. There wasn't anything that unusual about having old ladies I didn't know ask about it.

I wished Jason were there. Everyone knows he loves to freak old ladies out, and these old ladies seemed like they could really use a good scare. But I couldn't think of anything to do to them offhand, so I made the sign of the cross with my fingers. I don't know what that's supposed to do, but in horror movies, that's what you're supposed to do when you see a vampire or a werewolf or something. And I was starting to get the idea that these old ladies were just as scary as any movie monster.

But they didn't react to the cross, so I just ran like crazy around into my backyard, and went in through the back door and up to my room. It was a long time before I had enough nerve to look out the window to see if they were still there. Thankfully, they were gone. Within about an hour, I'd recovered enough that I could wish I'd played some sort of prank on them. Creepy old ladies who go around suggesting that people pull dirty tricks to keep people out of spelling bees deserve to get pranked, or I don't know who does.

That was when I called you to tell you everything they'd said, Chrissie.

I called Jennifer, too, to warn her to be on the lookout for old ladies who had something against her. She practically cried when I told her—I guess she had enough to worry about without having to worry about crazy old ladies, too.

Something was really messed up in town. Messed up enough that weird old ladies were taking to the streets. And they were up to no good.

This town needed something to cut the tension.

Something like a belch to end all belches.

26
JENNIFER

renounce—verb. To give up a claim, belief, or position formally. *Jennifer was prepared not only to give up the spelling bee, but to renounce spelling altogether and spend the rest of her life misspelling everything.*

I found out early on Thursday that Marianne was actually trying to get the school to ratify her "war" against me. She had actually issued a formal declaration of war! Like, maybe she thought she could actually get permission to lob a grenade at me if she got Floren to sign the right form! That girl would probably LOVE military school.

They sent us both to talk to Mrs. McGovern, the guidance counselor, who made us sit around talking in "I messages." An "I message" is a sentence in which you say "I feel (blank) when you (blank), and I want (blank) because (blank)." I thought it sounded pretty robotic, though I could imagine that Marianne would think putting that much structure and rules into complaining was really super.

My "I message" was "I feel bad when you accuse me

of cheating, and I want you to leave me alone because I'm not cheating."

Hers was "I feel that you're a disgrace to spelling when you claim that you don't have the word list, and I want you to surrender because you're a cheater. S-U-R-R-E-N-D-E-R. Surrender."

Mrs. McGovern then went into her speech about whether we wanted to be known as "warm fuzzies" or "cold pricklies," but I sort of tuned out, since I'd heard her give that speech a dozen times before. After that, they gave us both playground monitors, women whose normal job was to keep kids from cracking their heads open at recess, to act like bodyguards or something, and I went back to my routine of just ignoring her. I was ignoring everything in class by then. Even Mutual. I just sat there and recited Shakespeare lines over and over in my head and concentrated on that instead. It helped a lot.

I tromped through the snow like never before on my way home the day before the bee. I dove face-first into drifts and rolled around. I even intentionally shoved snow down into my clothes. I was freezing cold and soaking wet and aching all over when I got home. My mother was upset, of course, but the faces she made were really terrific, and it gave her something to yell about besides spelling for a minute.

After I got changed into dry clothes, she came into my room and told me, very softly, that she and Dad didn't want to push me or put too much pressure on me in regards to the bee (ha! I wonder which magazine for hyperactive parents told her to say THAT!). They just wanted me to get into a good college and get a good job. Then she told me that all of those other kids were my enemies, and should be shown no mercy.

I thought about telling her that I wasn't sure how much winning a spelling bee would actually help me get a job. And I thought about telling her that these were my friends, and the fact that we had to compete against each other in a spelling bee didn't make them all into bitter enemies of mine. But instead I just politely told her that I was under a lot of stress and needed to be left alone to concentrate, and that I'd be up in my room the whole night. They could come in to bring me some dinner, but, other than that, I was not to be disturbed. This meant that I'd be skipping *all* of my normal Thursday evening activities. She didn't argue.

But I didn't exactly get any peace and quiet, because my phone rang off the wall that night. Reporters were calling. Relatives were calling. Even Harlan called to say some creepy old ladies were out to get me, which was about the last thing I needed, even though I was pretty sure it was just one of his pranks.

This was one more thing that I didn't need. Part of me didn't want to win the bee because some creep out there wanted me to win so much that he had helped Dad organize a break-in. But now there were apparently a couple of freaky old ladies who wanted me to lose—I didn't want them to get what they wanted, either.

The only thing I could do was forget about everyone else in town and what they thought, and just win that bee for myself. Then I could drop a couple of activities and stay out of military school. And, in the process, beat Marianne and impress Mutual.

I couldn't wait for the bee to be over. I know some kids in class had looked forward to their chance to be competitors in the bee all their lives, but I just wanted it to end.

Still, over the previous couple of weeks, I had managed to get out of flute lessons, Spirit Squad, the recycling club, the Just Say No Club, Junior Farmers, Junior Motivational Speakers, and indoor soccer. As upset as I was, it was hard not to think of it as one of the best weeks of my life, in a way.

27
MUTUAL

synonym—noun. A word that means the same thing as another word in the same language. *"Rear" is a popular synonym for "buttocks."*

The evening before the bee, my parents made me "do" words most of the night. It seemed strange to me that this had been my favorite thing to do only days before. Now I did the words dutifully, but I spent the whole evening wanting to go to my room and listen to Paranormal Execution, whose songs were running in my head as though the player Jason loaned me had been implanted in my brain. My parents had once told me that certain songs were written in a tricky manner that made them get into your head—they were not quite sure of how this was accomplished, but it was said to involve Druidic manuscripts discovered by the Brickcutters.

I no longer believed this. I had received the music from Jason Keyes, and I trusted his judgment. He may have acted like a corrupt troublemaker, but, deep down, he was a noble student whose bravery had gotten him a girlfriend.

They had been right, however, about the tricks and manners of many people in the outside world. I was steering clear of Marianne Cleaver as much as possible—she sort of frightened me. And there were lots of rumors that Principal Floren himself was corrupt—I still did not understand why he had given me the sloppily written list of spelling words, but, based on the way that Chrissie Woodward was acting, I suspected foul play. Plus Harlan Sturr had been sneaking up behind me all afternoon on Thursday, for some reason. I had no idea what he was up to.

As we sat at the dinner table, my mother asked me to do "compendium," "solvency," "fiscal," and "rigmarole." When I did those correctly, she asked for "suspicious."

"Suspicious," I said. "Adjective. Inclined to believe that something is wrong. As in 'I was suspicious of Principal Floren in regard to the spelling bee. S-U-S-P-I-C-I-O-U-S. Suspicious."

"Excellent," said Mother. "Are you really suspicious of him?"

"There are lots of rumors," I said, "that he authorized the break-in."

"Makes sense to me," said Mother. "You will show them all tomorrow, Mutual. You will show them how much better it is to be educated the old-fashioned way, like children were educated back in the good old days. You will come in first, then sweep the districts, then win the nationals! We will show them all!"

I was, in fact, determined to win the bee. If I did not at least qualify for districts, I would surely be pulled from Gordon Liddy. I would not be able to hang out with Jason and Amber anymore. And I would probably never see Jennifer again.

I had to win the bee.

28
CHRISSIE

Excerpt from notebook #32:
They sure don't do a lot of cleaning at the Burger Baron, and there's almost never anyone eating there. How do they stay in business?

Thursday. January 31. The night before Bee Day.

I felt like I was getting closer to figuring out what was wrong with the faculty.

The recording I stole of the previous Thursday night cleared up a lot for me. It showed Floren making a phone call to someone named Mitch—obviously Jennifer's dad—followed by about eighteen minutes of fuzz. Floren had apparently tried to erase that conversation from the recording, but, well, technology just wasn't his strong point. He had missed erasing enough of it to give him away. My guess was that sometime during those eighteen minutes, he had given Mitch Van Den Berg the combination to the locked filing cabinet and told him to go ahead with the break-in.

But it didn't all make sense. He had given Mutual a word

list. Why was he also helping Jennifer? And why was he recording himself in the office like that in the first place?

I just hoped that, in the time I had left before the end of the bee, I could put the rest of the pieces together. I didn't want to present all my evidence if I didn't know the motive, and time was running out. I imagined myself being in a cop movie, on the verge of being fired for playing by my own rules. And the chief was giving me twenty-four hours to solve the case and prove that I was a good detective, which they always do in movies.

But on Friday morning, Mutual finally remembered to bring me the list that Floren had given him. I took one look at it, and the last pieces of the puzzle started to fall into place.

The list was full of misspelled words.

Floren wasn't trying to help Mutual. He was trying to sabotage him by giving him a messed-up word list!

So now I knew that he wanted Jennifer to win. And he was so determined that Mutual lose that he was resorting to sabotage.

I just needed to know why.

29
JENNIFER

camaraderie—noun. A feeling of especially close trust and friendship among a particular group. *The students who had been involved in the Three-Bean Casserole War and the other events that led to the Great November Food Fight felt a certain camaraderie that lasted a lifetime.*

After I disappeared into my room on Thursday, the only communication I had with my family at all was an e-mail from Val that they printed up and slipped under the door. I found it Friday morning.

```
Hey, sport!
Tomorrow's the big bee! I know you can
do it! Bummer that Dad got in trouble,
huh? Just do your best, beleive in your-
self, and reach for the stars!
```

See? It's like she just copied a bunch of motivational posters. And she spelled "believe" wrong! Like I said. She learned to spell just long enough to get through the bees, then forgot everything.

> I remember my sixth-grade year in the bee—people in town wouldn't leave me alone! The night before, a couple of weird old ladies came up to me while I walked home and made me spell about fifty words! Good luck! I hope I can make it home some weekend soon!

I was so busy thinking about how unlikely it was that she'd come home soon—she almost never did—that it took me a moment to remember the night before when Harlan had told me that a couple of old ladies were out to get me. I hoped it was just a coincidence, and that it really was one of Harlan's pranks. What else could I do? Call the cops and ask them to pick up any old ladies they saw on the street?

On Bee Day, I crawled out of bed at five o'clock in the morning, and left for school at six. That's an hour before I normally left, and half an hour before my parents would be getting out of bed. That way I could get ready for class and walk to school in peace without anyone asking me to spell anything. I really don't think that getting through breakfast without having to spell the names of any gross diseases is too much to ask, but I had to be sneaky to manage it.

I wandered through the snow, expecting the school to be deserted at that hour, but, as it turned out, it was full of news vans and reporters, all standing around in the cold, drinking coffee. There were a couple of guys with TV cameras and radio stuff every year, but this was ridiculous. There were crews from Shaker Heights and Cornersville Trace. Apparently all the crap with Floren and my dad had made it a bigger story than ever.

In addition to them, there were a bunch of people from around town. Old people who didn't have kids, even. People who were just really into the school spelling program. I looked around for freaky old ladies, like the ones Harlan warned me about, but I didn't see any.

"Hey!" one of the reporters shouted. "Can we have a word with you?"

"No," I called out. "Not until the end of the bee!"

In the twenty minutes that I had to stand around outside before Mr. Ruggles came and unlocked the front door of the school, nine other reporters came up and tried to talk to me—I felt like a celebrity or something. I didn't talk to any of them, even though I would have loved to tell them all about the None of the Above school of studying ahead of time.

But they were all pretty nice—they even formed a sort of human wall in front of me so that none of the people from town could come up and bug me. I did take the cup of hot chocolate that one of them brought to me, though. I was freezing, after all, and I knew that that first sip of hot chocolate would feel too incredibly super to pass up. And it did. Just like putting on warm socks after walking around in the snow—all the cold inside me just melted away. There's something about hot chocolate that just makes everything right with the world. I even asked for another cup to give to my playground monitor/bodyguard when she showed up.

Everyone was in class on time that day, and everyone was reading dictionaries. Everyone except for Chrissie, of course, who was still busy scribbling things down in her notebook, and Harlan, who was hanging around Mutual for some reason.

Marianne kept pushing her playground monitor around, telling her exactly where to stand so that no one could look off of her dictionary, then making her move again five seconds later. As upset as I was at her, I couldn't help feeling sorry for her. The poor girl clearly has some serious issues.

A minute or so before class started, my playground monitor/bodyguard stepped away for a second to speak into a walkie-talkie, then stepped back over to me.

"Jennifer," she said softly, "I just thought I should tell you that your parents called the police and asked them to issue a warrant for the arrest of Marianne's parents."

"Why?" I asked.

"They didn't see you this morning," she said, "and assumed you'd been kidnapped. But since we can assure them that you're here, I'm sure they'll call it off."

If I could have crawled into my desk, I would have done it. They should really make desks big enough that you can hide inside them.

Mrs. Boffin came into the class precisely the moment school began, and started the day as she always did.

"Good morning, class," she said.

"G-O-O-D M-O-R-N-I-N-G, M-I-S-S-U-S B-O-F-F-I-N," said Marianne.

"Here it is," said Mrs. Boffin, sweetly. "The day that you've all been waiting for. As far as I know, everyone has done a fine job of avoiding all of the press so far today, and I want to thank you all for that. And no matter what happens today, I want to congratulate each and every one of you on all of the hard work that you've done to prepare for the bee.

"The bee will begin directly after lunch, but those of you who are in the bee will be eating backstage. Lunch will be provided by the Burger Baron."

Lots of kids cheered—everyone knows the food there is gross, but any meal that doesn't involve the three-bean casserole is something to get excited about around here. Strangely, I think Chrissie cheered the loudest. And she wasn't even in the bee. The whole morning, she had looked like she was about to explode. She was scribbling so fast that I half expected to see smoke coming from her pencil.

"Prior to the bee itself," said Mrs. Boffin, "there will be a performance by the Good Times Gang in the auditorium. Immediately after they are finished, the bee will begin. Those of you who are participating are to report backstage in one hour. Until then, we will be continuing our discussion of explorers."

And, as though this wasn't the biggest day of the year, she just picked up a piece of chalk and started to write on the board about Ferdinand Magellan. I don't think a single kid was paying attention, though, and she didn't try to stop the kids who were reading out of dictionaries instead of taking notes.

An hour later, Mrs. Rosemary appeared at the door and said, "Spellers, will you please leave your dictionaries and other study aids at your desks and follow me?"

Practically everyone in the class—including Chrissie, I

noticed—followed her out of the classroom and down the hall. We stopped at the fourth- and fifth-grade rooms to pick up the handful of kids from there who'd be entering.

Mrs. Rosemary then led us to the backstage area and told us all to take a seat on the floor. I sat down between Harlan and Chrissie.

"I thought you didn't sign up," I whispered to Chrissie.

"Shh!" she said. "I'm sneaking in. There's some data I still need to get."

Harlan then leaned over my lap to talk to Chrissie.

"Are you still going to be by the soundboard?" he asked.

"Yeah," said Chrissie. "But . . ."

"Don't worry," said Harlan. "If I get nervous, I'll just imagine everyone in their underwear. I'm sure you know how well that works." He smirked a bit.

"Any progress on that, by the way?" asked Chrissie.

"Not yet," said Harlan. "But I'm on it. If I don't find out today, I'll keep working on it next week."

"Assuming he's still here," said Chrissie.

I'm not into secrets the way Chrissie is, but I sure would have liked to know what the heck they were talking about. I was about to ask when Mrs. Rosemary stood up in front of us to start her speech.

"Spellers, I need your attention, please," she said. "You will have the rest of the morning to talk quietly and prepare yourselves for the bee. At eleven o'clock, you will be served lunch. At eleven-thirty, the Good Times Gang will perform for twenty minutes, and you may listen to them via the intercom system. You will be led to your places at exactly noon for the beginning of the bee. When you are called, you will go to the microphone. You may ask for the definition of your word, or the root word, or language of origin, and you can ask for it to be used in a sentence. If you miss, a bell will ring, and you will take a seat in the auditorium. When a round ends with five or fewer spellers remaining, those five will be qualified for the district bee. If a round ends with no spellers remaining, everyone eliminated that round will be called back up. Are there any questions?"

"How come you're letting HER enter?" Marianne asked, pointing at me. "She has the list!"

"No one has the list," said Mrs. Rosemary. "In fact, we are not using our own master list. We are borrowing a list from Shaker Heights, just to make sure there can be no accusations of cheating. Any other questions?"

No one raised their hand.

Mrs. Rosemary smiled, wished us all great luck, and told us that we'd have the next hour to "reflect quietly on the bee, your studies, and what you hope to accomplish." She walked out, still smiling brightly.

I leaned over to Chrissie. "Have you ever seen her not smiling?"

"Nope," she said.

People got up from the floor and started milling about. Marianne started walking over toward me, but our playground monitors both stood in her way, so she scribbled something down on a sheet of paper and passed it over to Brittany, who passed it to a fifth grader, who passed it to me. For a second I thought she was going to offer a truce, and we could be back to being acquaintances, if not exactly friends, and quit being enemies, but the note said:

Jennifer,
I just wish for you to know that, even though there has been no formal declaration of war, it is ON.
Marianne

I wadded up the note, smiled, nodded, and threw it into the trash.

I walked over to the wall and sat down, leaning up against it and trying to just shut my brain off before it could get me all upset. Out on the stage, we could hear them setting up the sound equipment, with the terrible rumbles and wailing feedback, coupled with the occasional shouts of the reporters, cameramen, and radio guys trying to get the best spots they could to do their jobs. Brittany Tatomir came up and sat next to me.

"Crazy, huh?" said Brittany.

"Yeah," I said with a sigh. "I'm just glad it's all going to be over after today. What are you going to do when it's all over?" I asked.

"I'm going down to the Quickway," she answered, "and getting a tall, frosty orange soda. One of those enormous ones that only cost a nickel more than the mediums. And all the gum I can afford. How about you?"

"Personally," I said, "I'm going to run through the snow, get soaking wet and freezing cold, then have a superhuge glass of hot chocolate with marshmallow cream."

"Yeah?" said Tony Ostanek, turning around and joining us. "Won't you still be busy studying for districts tonight?"

"Heck no," I said. "I'm gonna need a break. Assuming I

qualify at all. And I have a new studying system that isn't really studying, exactly, anyway. It's just . . . learning stuff."

"Weird," said Tony. "Hope it works for you!"

"How about you, Tony?" Brittany asked. "What are you going to do when this whole spelling bee thing is over?"

"I tell ya," said Tony, "I've been so busy studying, I'm afraid I'm losing my knack for games. I'm going to go home, kiss my television, and play video games on her until she overheats." He pulled out his wallet and took out a photo of a big TV. "See that?" he asked, pointing to it proudly. "That's her. That's what I'm spelling for. A new game just for being here, and three if I win."

"That sounds nice," said Jake Wells, moving over to talk to us. "That sounds really nice. Sometimes we forget why we're spelling, huh?"

"What are you going to do after it's over, Jake?" I asked.

"Hey," said Jake, wistfully. "I'm no great student or nothing, I'm just a kid who eats things for dollars. I'd like to win that gift certificate and all, but it's a long shot. All I know is that, as a student, it's my right to compete in the all-school bee, and I'm proud to be here, win or lose. And when it's over, I'm going to eat a great big hamburger. Medium rare, so it's a bit charred on the outside, but pink all through the middle. With mustard, lettuce, ketchup, onions, pickles, and a toasted bun, with a chocolate malt."

"We're getting burgers for lunch," I said.

"Yeah," said Jake. "But I'm talking about a great big one. Not fast food. One thing about eating nasty stuff for a living is that you learn to appreciate the finer things when you can get them. And that stuff from the Burger Baron ain't finer than nothing!"

We all smiled and passed around the picture of Tony's TV set. More people came over to talk about their plans for after the bee. Even Amber and Tony seemed to be acting friendly toward each other, and just a few days earlier he'd been calling her a witch. It was a really nice feeling—we were all about to be rivals, going head to head, and we could hear the sounds of the battle being set up right behind the wall, but for right then, we were all friends. It was like something out of a Shakespeare play.

At eleven o'clock, a couple of old ladies wandered in, pushing a cart with the Burger Baron logo on it.

"Ooh!" I heard Jason say. "Old ladies!"

"Watch out, Jennifer!" I heard Chrissie shout.

If you've never been in a position where the world was going crazy to start with, but then you hear that old ladies were out to get you, and then a couple of old ladies walk into the room, well . . . you'll never know what I felt like right then. Sometimes you hear people say their blood turned to ice, right? Well, it really does feel like that. Like everything inside you is suddenly frozen.

The old ladies wheeled the cart up to the front of the room and smiled at us. Their teeth looked like little kernels of moldy corn. And they were looking right at me. Both of them.

"Good morning, spellers," one of them said. "Principal Floren has graciously allowed us to come bring you lunch." And both of them started laughing, which sounded like two chalkboards being rubbed together with fingernails in between them. It was a hideous, frightening sound.

"Do you have a visitor pass?" my playground monitor asked them.

"Tut, tut," said one of the ladies. "Surely you don't think a couple of old ladies are up to no good, do you?"

"If you don't have one," said the monitor, "then you need to go to the office and get one."

"In good time," said one of the ladies. "First we need to talk to our little spellers!"

A few kids groaned. "Little spellers"? Did they think we were five? Somehow this only made them scarier to me. It made it seem like they didn't have a firm grasp on reality, which meant they were a couple of nuts. Possibly a couple of *dangerous* nuts.

One of the old ladies pulled a little black book out of her purse and opened it up.

"Mutual Scrivener," she said, reading a name out of the book. "Is Mutual here?"

Mutual very meekly raised his hand.

"Are you feeling like a good speller today, Mutual? Studied the way you should have? Because I have a feeling that if you lose, there could be real trouble!"

"Shut up, Helen!" shouted one of the old ladies. "You're going to ruin everything!"

"I know what I'm doing, Agnes!" shouted the other one. "I'm just making sure little Mutual is in good shape today! You're the one who ought to shut up!"

"*You* should, you limp-livered old ninny!" the first one shouted.

I overheard the recess monitors muttering and looking nervous—they didn't seem to like the old ladies any more than I did.

Mutual, meanwhile, sat still, looking terrified. Mutual had probably never seen anyone so creepy; the poor kid was probably just about ready to wet his pants. I understood.

"Madam, please," said my playground monitor. "No one without a visitor pass is allowed to harass the students."

"No one is doing any harassing," said the other old lady.

Mutual's lower lip was trembling. I saw him lean over and say something to Jason, and Jason said something back.

"And Jennifer?" said one of them. "Is Jennifer Van Den Berg here?"

I didn't raise my hand. I ducked my head between my knees and tried to hide.

"Excuse me, ladies," said Jason, standing up. "But I'll speak for Mutual. He's in perfect shape today!" He was speaking in a superpolite voice. I poked my head back up to see what he was up to.

"Wonderful," said the first old lady. She opened her mouth to say something else, but Jason stayed standing up and started walking up toward them. Everyone had heard him talk about how he loved to freak old ladies out, but this was the first time I, for one, had ever actually seen him in action.

"Let me be the first to welcome you both to Gordon Liddy," he said. "I'm Jason Keyes, student body president."

"You are not!" shouted Marianne. We don't actually have a student body president. If we did, Marianne would be all over that gig.

"He is too!" shouted Harlan, laughing and playing along with him. Harlan jumped up to stand next to Jason. "I'm Captain Harlan Sturr, deputy chief of staff to President Keyes." He bowed deeply.

The recess monitors looked at each other and sort of half shrugged. Their jobs were to guard me and Marianne from each other, not to guard old ladies from Jason and Harlan. From the looks on their faces, I'd say that they were almost relieved that someone was standing up to Helen and Agnes. They seemed a bit confused as to what to do about them.

Everyone sort of snickered as Jason walked closer and closer. "On behalf of the school," he continued, "I'd like to thank you for attending the spelling bee. We're always happy to entertain a couple of geezers."

"Young man!" shouted Helen. "In my day, we did not refer to our elders as geezers!"

"President Keyes is terribly sorry," Harlan said, smiling. "But, in answer to your question, Mutual has studied hard, and is ready to kick some serious butt. So don't you geezers worry!"

"I beg your pardon!" said Agnes. "In my day, you'd have been paddled across your behinds!"

I'd never seen anyone so upset over the word "geezers." I guess she was surprised to hear it from a "little speller."

"Paddled?" said Harlan. "Well, be my guest!"

And he turned his back to them, bent over, and unbuttoned his jeans like he was going to moon them.

Everyone gasped, and a lot of people laughed. I couldn't help giggling myself, especially when he put his thumbs into the belt loops and started to act like he was actually going to pull down the back of his pants. It looked like he was really going to do it!

"Yeah, I think we both need it!" said Jason. And he turned around and acted like he was going to moon them, too!

"Come on, guys!" said Harlan. "Everybody get up!"

Tony got up. Then Gunther did. Then Mutual, who looked very nervous, stood up. Harlan gave him a nod of encouragement. Most of the kids who were sitting were practically cracking up.

I felt like I was watching history unfold. This was the kind of thing that kids would tell their younger siblings about—the day that all the guys had mooned a couple of old ladies before the spelling bee!

Harlan was the first to actually lower the back of his pants. I don't think anyone but the old ladies could actually see any more than a glimpse of his boxers, but we were all in hysterics. Then Jason lowered his even further. I looked over at the recess monitors, who looked like deer caught in headlights. Mutual looked sort of confused, but he followed suit, unbuckling his belt and starting to undo his slacks.

Now, let me make this clear, since I know that there are a lot of stories going around about what happened—no one ACTUALLY mooned the old ladies. A couple of the guys lowered the backs of their pants an inch or two, but that's all. It was enough to freak the old ladies out. They made horrified faces at each other and started backing up.

The recess monitors jumped into action. They ran up to the old ladies while they were too busy being stunned to argue and hustled them out the door and into the hallway.

In the process, Helen dropped the black book she had been holding, and I noticed that Chrissie jumped forward and grabbed it.

When the recess monitors came back in—alone—a second later and locked the door, everyone applauded.

I'm sure that in years to come, the story will get changed around as kids retell the story over and over. We've all heard stories like the one about Johnny Dean painting Principal Floren's dog purple, but I don't think I'd ever actually witnessed the sort of event that would go down in school history. Not until then.

This would make legends out of some of us. Maybe all of us.

Jason rebuttoned his pants and bowed. Harlan and Mutual followed. Everyone applauded and laughed. One of the recess monitors went over and scolded them a little, but you could see that her heart wasn't in it. It was some time before things calmed down, but, when they did, it felt even more like there was a spirit of camaraderie in the room. I was proud to be spelling with these people. They might not have been just like me, but they were my friends. All of them.

Well, all except Marianne, of course. She spent the whole episode sitting in the corner, scowling like a regular little troll. I smiled over at her, and she looked so mad that I thought that she was going to jump up and attack me.

Meanwhile, Chrissie was sitting in the corner, reading through the little black book they had dropped. Then she shouted, "Aha!" and ran out of the room—I had to wonder what the heck had been in that book.

The recess monitors told us not to touch the burgers the

old ladies had brought in, which was fine with us. I would have sooner eaten candy from a stranger. Instead they put in a call to a pizza place that was able to bring us a whole stack of pizzas in fifteen minutes.

Through the intercom, I could hear the Good Times Gang starting into their opening number, a song called "It's Cool to Stay in School." They were booked at least once a year—they did a lot of songs about why smoking and drinking were bad, why you should listen to your parents, and how to cope with peer pressure. Things like that.

You know what? The chorus of "It's Cool to Stay in School" actually sort of says that you *should* listen to peer pressure.

> Now I'm a homeless junkie and
> I live on crumbs and gruel
> 'Cause no one ever told me that
> It's cool to stay in school.

See? The reason the guy in the song ended up a junkie is that there was no peer pressure to stay in school!

We all knew the words by then, since they hadn't changed their act in years. So we sang along as loudly as we could, laughing our heads off. The next song was called "My Aunt Judith Smokes," and we sang along with that, too, while we ate our pizza.

It was as good a way as any to keep our minds off the fact that the bee would be starting in less than twenty minutes. We were going to have to stop being friends and go out on-stage to be enemies.

30
MUTUAL

rosaceous—adjective. Resembling a rose.
Most kids would blush so hard at the very thought of
showing an old lady their butt that they would be
positively rosaceous.

I freely admit that I was terrified when the old ladies showed up and began to ask me questions. How did they know who I was? Why did they care if I felt like a good speller? Why were they spitting? Were they going to spit on me? And what did they mean when they said there would be trouble if I did not win?

While they were shouting at each other, I leaned over to Jason and muttered, "Help!" I was too scared to say anything else. Jason had leaned over and said, "I'm on it."

Over the previous two weeks, he had spent lots of time talking about different ways of frightening old ladies—but I had certainly never seen him do so before. In fact, I was coming to the conclusion that he just liked to *talk* about freaking old ladies out, but never actually did it.

Watching him and Harlan get up and prepare to

frighten the old ladies had been an inspiring sight. The applause in the room afterward was like nothing I had ever experienced. I felt as though I was a part of something bigger than myself, and it felt wonderful.

Amber was blushing. "I can't believe how brave you guys were!" she said to us. "I'm going to cast a spell for both of you right now!"

And she spun around three times, then sat cross-legged on the floor and started chanting intently.

"Thank you, Jason," I said. "If you had not stood up, no one would have."

"Hey, man," he said. "No old ladies freak people out on my watch. Sometimes we have to help each other out, right? But Harlan was the one who started mooning them. That was brilliant."

He looked over to Harlan, and pointed at him. Harlan pointed back, smiling.

Shortly thereafter, I got my very first taste of pizza. It immediately became my favorite food of all time. It was further proof to me that the outside world was not nearly as bad as my parents had told me. No place that has pizza can be all bad.

Just about then, the sound of what I assumed was the Good Times Gang came over the intercom. The first song appeared to be called "It's Cool to Stay in School," which was more like a campfire song than a metal song, but it must have been very popular, since all the other students were singing along and laughing boisterously.

The next song, about a woman who dies of smoking, was equally well received. I particularly enjoyed the third number, which they said was called "Get High on Self-Esteem." After the last song, "If Y'All Wanna Join a Gang, Join the Good Times Gang!" they explained that we were all now honorary members of the Good Times Gang, and that, if we were ever asked to cheat, steal, drink, or do drugs, we could just say "Hey! I don't need to do that stuff! I'm a member of the Good Times Gang!"

I suppose it was an honor, even though I'd been raised not to use terms such as "hey," and had been warned all my life never to join any gangs. Everyone else in the school had probably been made an honorary member years ago, though, and I was glad to catch up. They were a gang of good guys, not a gang of hoodlums, after all. If there were bad gangs around, it stood to reason that there must have been good ones to stop them.

As soon as the Gang left the stage, Mrs. Rosemary came in and led us out of the backstage area and into the auditorium, where the bee itself would take place. I had waited for this moment for most of my life.

I had to squint for a second when I first stepped out onto the stage, since the lights were so bright. When I took my seat on the risers that were set up on the stage, my eyes began to adjust, and I could see that every seat was filled with a student or teacher, except for the first two rows. That, Mrs. Rosemary explained, was where we were to go sit when we missed a word.

There were cameras filming things in the aisles, and another camera was set up right behind the little booth in the middle of the audience where the man running the sound was. Back behind us, a very large screen was set up, showing the microphone. I guessed that it would be showing a large video image of whoever was spelling at the time.

Mrs. Rosemary came out to give a little speech to the audience about how this was not really a competition, but a celebration of spelling, education, town pride, and self-esteem. I leaned over to Jason.

"She is not telling the truth, right?" I asked. "Because if this is not a competition, my parents will be very upset."

"Nah," said Jason. "It's just the speech she gives every year. It's a competition, all right."

When Mrs. Rosemary finished, a woman from Hedekker's Appliance Store gave a speech about how the store liked to give back to the community. After that, a man at the judges' table, which was set up on the side of the stage, called Amber Hexam to be the first speller.

Amber slowly rose from her seat, still chanting under her breath. She had been rocking back and forth, and, when she opened her eyes, I noticed that they were crossed. She looked rather dizzy as she made her way up to the microphone.

I looked back to see the video image of her at the microphone. If she had seemed dizzy walking to the microphone, her close-up made her look as though she'd been hit by a truck.

"Amber," said the man at the table, "your word is 'pithecan.'"

"Man, they're starting out tough!" said Jason.

"Can . . ." She shook her head, then held it in her hands. "Sentence?" she asked.

"What is wrong with her?" I muttered to Jason.

"She must have chanted too hard and given herself a headache!" he whispered back.

"'Pithecan,'" said the man at the desk, "means of or relating to apes. As in 'Neanderthals were pithecan.'"

Behind me, I heard Harlan giggle. "As in 'Principal Floren is pithecan!'" he said.

"Pithecan," Amber repeated, slowly. "P-I-T-H-A—"

The bell rang.

Amber shook her head and slowly walked down to the front row of seats, where she sat down, looked at Jason, then shrugged.

"I guess her plan backfired," I said.

"Guess so," said Jason. "That can happen. If you focus or concentrate too hard, you can end up feeling like your brain is melting. It's up to you and me now."

Jennifer was next, and she correctly spelled "apostate." Then Marianne got "rosaceous," which she spelled correctly. The next person was a fourth grader who misspelled "beagle."

Jason's first word, believe it or not, was "malodorous." Of course he got that one right—any Paranormal Execution fan would know that one!

Harlan was next, and got the word "soubresaut."

"Soubresaut," Harlan repeated, slowly. "Soubresaut . . . what the heck does that mean?"

"It's a ballet term," said the man at the table. "Meaning a type of jump that begins and ends with the feet in a closed position."

"Well, no kidding?" Harlan asked. "What's the language of origin?"

"French."

"Can you use it in a sentence?"

"Certainly." The judge cleared his throat. "The ballerina executed a perfect soubresaut."

"Okay," said Harlan. "Soubresaut." He paused, then casually said, "How do you spell that?"

The man at the desk opened his mouth, then shook his head and said, "Nice try, kid."

Everyone snickered, and Harlan bowed, then spelled the word correctly.

Then they called my name. This was it—my first word in a real spelling bee. All of the thousands of words my parents had made me do over the years had been in anticipation of this moment.

I rose from the riser and walked up to the microphone. I took a quick glance back to see myself on the large screen, but all I could see by doing that was the back of my head.

Suddenly I was incredibly nervous. After all this, what if I missed the word? My whole life would have been a waste.

"Mutual," said the man at the table. "Your first word is 'choreutic.'"

"Choreutic," I said. "Adjective. Belonging to a chorus in a song. As in 'The choreutic sections of the songs of the Good Times Gang were very catchy.'"

Lots of people giggled, and I felt a bit less stressed, and rather flattered to have made the people laugh. This, I thought, must be how Harlan felt when he cracked wise.

"That's correct," said the man at the table. "But you don't need to supply the definition, only the spelling."

"C-H-O-R-E-U-T-I-C. Choreutic," I said.

"Correct," the man said.

I went back to my seat, feeling greatly relieved, and Jason patted me on the back. The next speller, a fifth grader, missed "barathrum." The following three spellers were eliminated as well.

If things continued at this rate, the spelling bee would not last long.

31
CHRISSIE

Excerpt from notebook #27:
After school, Jake Wells often shoots baskets with
Floren. Neither is very good at it.

I understood everything now. When the old lady dropped
her little black book, I'd only needed to look at it for a second to solve the whole mystery.

The little black book was a list of who had bet how
much money on which speller. The old ladies ran some sort
of gambling ring! According to the book, a whole bunch of
people had made bets on the bee.

Floren had bet on Jennifer—he had probably set up the
break-in so that he could help her win. By not just GIVING
her father the list, he could say that he hadn't been involved! And he probably would have gotten away with it—
except that I had the footage of him making the call to set
the whole thing up!

The old ladies probably wanted Mutual to win—no one
in town had bet on him, so they wouldn't have to pay

anyone off if he came in first. That's why they were so interested in whether he was a good speller!

With the messed-up list, the black book, and the recordings, I had plenty of evidence to get Floren fired. And, since everyone in town would be watching on TV, I'd be able to present it to all of them at the same time! And the cameras from other towns would probably pick up the story, so everyone in the tricounty area would know about it!

I knew there would be more media present at the bee than normal, but what was going on was ridiculous. Cameras everywhere, and a jumbo screen behind the stage showing a close-up of the current speller. It looked more like a rock concert than a small-town spelling bee. I looked around and figured out which camera was taping the views shown on the screen—information like that was sure to come in handy later. If I put one of the discs into the camera, that could override the system. Instead of showing the stage, the big screen would show whatever was on the disc.

I was ready to act. I just had to wait for the right moment.

Onstage, spellers were dropping like flies. As usual, the fourth and fifth graders were eliminated pretty quickly. Only a couple of them made it into the second round, and then one of them actually missed "coffee," if you can believe that. I'm not sure if it was just nerves or what, but the poor kid looked pretty embarrassed to miss such an easy word. Right on television, too.

Jennifer and Marianne both plowed their way through the first couple of rounds, of course, and so did Mutual.

Enough people got eliminated early that I was hearing people around me whisper that this was going to be a pretty short bee, but I knew better. Those three were likely to keep it going for quite a while.

I was especially impressed with Harlan. In the first round, I figured that he was toast when his word was "soubresaut," which is a ballet term, and I was really afraid that he'd be disqualified for trying the old "how do you spell that" routine, but he spelled it correctly and went on to round two. In the second round he got "turophile," a really fancy word for "one who really, really likes cheese," and nailed that, too.

And so it went for about an hour. Jason's second word was "obfuscate," which I supposed was a word he knew from metal songs, since he spelled it correctly right away and practically danced his way back to his seat on the risers.

After five or six rounds, they were down to just a handful of people, all of them sixth graders. Mutual, Jennifer, and Marianne were still in the running, of course. So was Brittany, which didn't surprise me much—she's smarter than she acts. Jason was still in the running, too, partly because he kept getting words that any self-respecting headbanger would probably know. That's a spelling bee for you—as much studying as it takes to get good at spelling, it really all comes down to luck.

Within an hour and a half, it was down to eight people.

Only three more people had to miss a word for Harlan to break into the top five.

On the next round, Tony missed "wallop," which he

thought was spelled "whallop." I would have made the same mistake myself.

Then Jason got "cheerful," which he spelled with two 'L's. He got the biggest applause of anyone when he took a seat next to Amber in the front row, especially from people who had been backstage and seen what he'd done there to freak the old ladies out.

I clapped for him as loudly as anybody. The mooning thing had really been Harlan's idea—only *I* knew that he was probably doing it as a ruse to help me confirm my suspicion that Mutual wore tighty-whities—but Jason had been the one who started messing with the old ladies in the first place. And if he hadn't come as close as he had to showing those old ladies his butt, giving the recess monitors a chance to hustle them out, they wouldn't have dropped the little black book, which gave me the last piece of evidence that I needed. He was a brave guy, and he deserved every bit of applause he got.

I was starting to wonder lately if Jason's acting up and getting in trouble wasn't based on his being a wannabe hoodlum so much as on him being brave. Being brave sort of comes naturally to some people, and there aren't many chances to exercise it in Preston. Maybe his attempts to get in trouble over the years were just his way of looking for adventure. I couldn't believe I hadn't figured that out before, given all the things I knew about him. Same with Harlan. I guess I'd never really thought about *why* he had become the class clown, and I never stopped to think of how admirable he was, in a way. I'd been too busy turning him in for breaking the rules.

Things really look different on the other side.

As Jason took his seat, I looked around for the old ladies—they were standing in the back of the room. One of them was spitting on the carpet. Principal Floren was standing next to them, and even in the dark room, I could see that he was sweating. He wasn't even *trying* to get them to stop spitting.

With Jason out, only six people remained onstage. Harlan only had a little further to go.

32
JENNIFER

malfunction—verb. To break down or fail to operate properly. *When something caused the robot to malfunction, it started shooting at itself, not the aliens.*

All through the bee, Marianne kept looking over at me and giving me dirty glances. I just smiled at her every time, and it drove her crazy. I could tell.

I was starting to feel good. Something about what went on backstage had just swept everything else away. I was feeling like myself again. Like the person I wanted to be. This is not to say that I didn't want to beat Marianne, though, because I certainly did. I was smiling at her, but only because I knew that saying "I'm gonna kick your butt so hard it'll come flying out of your mouth" was exactly what she wanted me to do. Smiling at her was driving her nuts. More than she normally was, even.

The first part of the bee went by pretty quickly. All the fourth and fifth graders went out inside of the first three rounds, and by round eleven, there were only six of us left:

me, Marianne, Mutual, Brittany, Jake, and Harlan. If anyone missed a word, everyone who survived the round would go to districts.

The six of us went through three more rounds without anybody missing a word. I got "bathyal," a term relating to the deepest parts of the ocean, "galleon," a kind of coin that pirates were into, and "sneezeweed," which I didn't ask for a definition on, but assumed was probably a weed that makes you sneeze. The None of the Above school of studying felt like it was working. I *felt* smarter, and that made me *act* smarter. Or more confident, anyway. And confidence is pretty important in a bee.

When Marianne was called up again at the end of round twelve, after the rest of us had spelled our words for the round correctly, she looked over at me and snarled as she got up. Over the last few rounds, she'd been breathing heavily, and looked like she might explode at any minute. When she snarled, I smiled back brightly, and for just a second she looked so furious at me that I thought her eyes might start glowing red, or that she would start breathing fire. I'm not sure I'd ever seen anyone so angry, and I've seen my mother when I put wet clothes on the furniture.

Marianne made her way up to the microphone, not swinging her arms, and still looking like a robot, but now looking like a very angry robot. I looked around behind me at the large TV screen that was showing close-ups of people and saw that she was practically seething. He eyes had gotten wide, and you could hear her breathing into the microphone quite loudly through the PA system. She was starting to look like one of those people on late-night religious TV who get possessed by demons.

"Your word," said the man at the desk, "is 'jocular.' "

"Jugular," Marianne repeated. "A vein. In the neck. As in 'I will stab you in the jugular.' "

"Um, no, 'jocular,' " said the guy. "As in . . ."

But Marianne wasn't listening.

"Jugular," she seethed. "J-U—"

The bell rang.

"Wait!" she shouted, suddenly panicking. She had totally missed!

I didn't dare look back at the screen to see the look on her face. Surely she would have known how to spell "jocular." But she had let the stress and the anger get to her—she had made a mistake, and though they'd made the attempt to correct her before she could screw up, she'd been too busy being PO'd to pay attention.

"I'm sorry," said the man at the desk. "But that's incorrect."

"No!" she howled. She stood still on the stage for a second; then Mrs. Rosemary came and led her away. She was out. And I breathed about the deepest sigh of relief in human history. Any deeper breath could probably have caused a hurricane or something.

The round was over, and only five of us remained.

Brittany, Harlan, Mutual, Jake, and I would be going to districts. There was some polite applause, and I could hear that Marianne was having a hissy fit, but I barely noticed. I was just staring up at the ceiling, smiling. As far as I was concerned, the real pressure was over. I'd beaten Marianne. I was going to districts. Even if I lost now, I could make up for it at districts. At least for the time being, there was no chance of military school or more activities!

There was a round of applause for those of us who remained. While Principal Floren gave a little speech about how the people onstage would be representing Preston at districts, I moved over and sat right by Mutual.

"Hi," I said.

"Hello," he said, looking at me.

"I read *Henry V*," I said. "It's part of how I studied for the bee."

I saw his eyes get really wide behind his glasses.

"You did not read a dictionary?" he asked.

"Nope," I said. "I just studied Shakespeare and looked up the words I didn't know. It's a new theory for how to study that I'm working on."

"That is very interesting," he said. "Perhaps we can read a play together when we study for districts."

"Sure," I said. And I smiled. And *he* smiled for a second, but then he blushed and looked away.

You know how people say they feel butterflies in their stomach? That's what it felt like. Like I'd swallowed a whole jar of butterflies. And not dead ones, either, which you would think most butterflies in jars would be. I'd felt it before, but usually it was nervousness—the kind the bee brought on, where it feels like the butterflies are flying all around in every direction in your stomach. These ones were all flying straight upward. Only they weren't coming out of my mouth or anything.

I know. It's weird. It's best not to think TOO hard about these things, or you'll go nuts.

Neither of us said much for a few seconds, but Floren was still going on about town pride, academic excellence, and blah, blah, blah. Mutual glanced back at me again once or twice. He tried to look like he wasn't smiling, but he was.

He liked me!

Finally Mutual leaned over to Harlan and said, "That was very brave, what you did in the backstage area."

"Think nothing of it," said Harlan. "You ain't seen nothing yet!"

"You are going to do something else?" he asked.

"Just watch," said Harlan. "You want brave, you'll get it!"

Floren finished his speech, and there was some light applause as the bee got back in gear. Most of the people in the auditorium had a sheet of paper and pen out, since their teachers would probably be making them learn every word that came up from here on out.

"Jennifer," the judge called, "you're up next."

I stood up, and smiled back at everyone.

"Once more unto the breach, dear friends," I said to them. That's a line from *Henry V*. Mutual smiled when I said it. The butterflies fluttered again.

But then, as I stepped to the mike, I thought I heard someone—looking back, I *think* it was Principal Floren, but I'm not sure—shouting, "Go, Jennifer!" and my blood froze again. All the butterflies in my stomach just died. Because of the frost caused by the frozen blood, I guess. That'll kill butterflies every time.

In a split second, I decided it was time to get out of the bee.

The creepy old ladies wanted me to lose, and I didn't want them to get what they wanted. But someone was still out there who wanted me to win. The two canceled each other out, in a way. I had decided not to worry about that stuff, and just win for my own sake, but it was a lot harder when I was actually up there, standing at the microphone. I'd forgotten all about it before, but now I was in districts, going for first place, which wouldn't get me anything more than the approval of my parents and a gift certificate I didn't really need. The idea of it being over and behind me felt a lot more appealing than the idea of winning.

I'd already beaten Marianne.

I had districts coming up, which meant I could get out of more activities. And I didn't suppose it mattered TOO much if I didn't win the bee, since I could still come in first at districts, which would redeem me to my parents.

And I'd already done well enough that I couldn't imagine I'd have to go to military school.

Heck. Even if I did have to go there, there couldn't be anything there that was any scarier than being confronted by those two old creeps.

Plus, I'd already apparently impressed Mutual enough with my spelling that he wanted to study with me. Maybe I could impress him more by doing something brave and letting someone who wanted it more win the bee!

"Jennifer," said the judge, "your word is 'remuneration.'"

"Remuneration," I repeated. "R-E-M-O—"

The bell rang.

Mutual would surely know I'd missed that on purpose. It wasn't a very hard word.

I waved back at the people on the risers as I walked to a seat in the auditorium, trying to look as brave and rebellious as I could, and took a seat next to Jason.

"Way to go!" he said. "I think you fried Marianne's brain!"

I looked back at the stage to see if Mutual looked impressed. He was still clapping for me, even though most people had stopped by then. I tried to keep from smiling TOO obviously as the butterflies started to come back to life. I winked at him, just to sort of show that I'd done it on purpose. He blushed again.

A few seconds later, Brittany spelled "remuneration" correctly, and the bee went on.

They called Harlan up to come spell his word, and he was beaming all the way to the microphone. He stood there for a second, scratching his nose and making weird motions with his hands toward the sound booth, where Chrissie was sitting.

"Harlan," said the man at the desk, "the word is 'obnoxious.'"

"Obnoxious," he said. I didn't know if it was just because of where I was sitting now or what, but suddenly the sound seemed to have been turned WAY up.

"Has it been this loud the whole time?" I whispered to Jason.

"No," said Jason. "It just got a lot louder."

"Obnoxious," Harlan repeated. "As in . . ."

He stepped back from the microphone for a second,

paused, then stepped back up, opened his mouth, and belched.

This was not just a casual belch, either. It was a big, loud, and long one. One of those burps that just keep going and going and going. For a few seconds, I even thought he might have been belching the National Anthem. With the microphone turned up as high as it was, it reverberated all through the auditorium so loudly that I wouldn't be surprised if the walls rattled. A couple of kids up front actually had to cover their ears.

It would have been one heck of a burp under any circumstances, and he'd done it into a mike at full volume, right at a critical moment in the spelling bee, when everyone was paying attention. Better yet, it had matched the definition of the word he was supposed to spell, in a way.

When the burp finally finished, the whole auditorium was deadly silent for a second; then just about every kid in the place jumped up and started cheering. One guy from the Good Times Gang even came out onstage and bowed deeply to Harlan. Everyone knew that we'd just witnessed an event that would go down in history.

Before the mooning thing, I hadn't witnessed any events that kids would talk about for years. Now I had seen two in one day. My dad always said that he never saw or thought about people he went to school with anymore. Obviously he'd never been through a day like this.

Harlan Sturr had just belched his way into becoming a hero. People wouldn't just tell stories about this—they would sing songs about it. I just knew that if I was to move to a hippie commune in Zanzibar and run into, say, Tony there fifty years from now, the first thing he would say would be "Remember when Harlan belched at the spelling bee?" And when Harlan dies, someone will probably tell this story at his funeral.

Onstage, Harlan was smiling and jumping up and down like he'd just won the entire bee, and pumping his fists into the air. Mrs. Rosemary had to come up onstage and start waving her hands to calm everybody down. When it was finally quiet enough, Harlan spelled the word correctly, and took his seat on the risers to thunderous applause.

33
MUTUAL

soubise—noun. An onion sauce. *The cafeteria lady said it was a soubise, but it was really just cheap canned gravy that had been watered down.*

I could not believe the immensity of the belch Harlan managed to emit into the microphone. It seemed to come from the very depths of his soul. The ovation the other students gave him seemed to go on for several minutes before Mrs. Rosemary could quiet everyone down. Harlan was jumping around as though he had won the entire bee.

When he finally spelled the word correctly, people applauded for him again as he took his seat. Up close, I could see that he was positively beaming. I had never seen anyone look so happy.

"Way to go!" Jake said.

"That was amazing," I said.

In the audience, Jason was pointing at Harlan and smiling again. Harlan pointed back, though it looked more like he was pointing at Chrissie to me.

I wished I could do something that brave. The thing

with the old ladies had been the only time I had ever tried anything like it. When people clapped for me, it had felt wonderful. And that was nothing compared to the ovation that Harlan had just received. I could only imagine how he must have felt.

These were not the sort of actions my parents had raised me for—as far as they were concerned, I was only there to win the bee. Obviously Jennifer, Jason, and Harlan had more noble purposes in mind than simply winning spelling bees. I was not sure why Jennifer had lost, but I was sure she had an excellent reason. Something moral. And my parents HAD raised me to be moral.

I had been very nervous when Jennifer had come to speak with me, but, to my surprise, she had seemed interested in spending time with me. Perhaps I would not need to start a heavy-metal band to impress her after all! Instead, she could teach me about Shakespeare.

I was suddenly in a very, very good mood. Not nervous at all. I had eaten pizza, witnessed several acts of bravery, joined the Good Times Gang, and qualified for districts. It was the greatest day of my life.

I spelled my next word correctly, and so did Jake. Brittany then missed the word "vicissitude," spelling it with only one S. Funnily enough, it meant "a change in luck," which I suppose you could say was what had just happened to her, causing her to miss the word. But she did not seem to mind, either. She happily walked down to the front row, smiling all the way. She was already in the district bee, after all.

Then there were three of us.

As she walked to her seat, I leaned over to Jake. "This is getting pretty intense," I said.

"Yeah," he said. "I can't believe I made it to districts! I never thought I could do that!"

"You have done very well," I said.

"I guess so," he said. "I just started thinking of spelling as, like, the recipe for a word, and I've gotten them all right! I might actually win that gift certificate! I could get that nonstick cookware set!"

Harlan spelled "vicissitude" correctly, keeping himself in the contest.

I then correctly spelled "Guernsey," which is a type of cow. Then Jake correctly spelled "periwig," which was a kind of antique wig.

Harlan's next word was "soubise."

"Ooh!" Jake said. "A food word! I *know* this one!"

Harlan must have heard, because he looked back at us, smiled, and nodded to Jake.

"Soubise," he said into the microphone. "S-E-W—"

The bell rang. Harlan shrugged and walked off the stage—the applause he got was nearly deafening. Clearly, no one had forgotten the belch, and I doubted that anyone would be forgetting it any time soon. But maybe only I knew that he had missed that word on purpose because he knew that Jake knew it. He had already had his moment of glory, and now, perhaps, he wanted Jake to have one, too.

As I walked to the microphone for my turn to spell the word, I thought about how brave Harlan and Jason had been. And Jennifer, too, though I wasn't sure why she had missed her word. Somehow, losing on purpose, for a good reason, seemed to be so much more respectable to me than simply trying to win. Judging by the applause that Harlan got, other people thought so, too.

As I stepped to the microphone, I made a decision.

It seemed that, since coming in first did not really put one in a better position to win the district bee, the only people who would really care if I came in first were my parents and the old ladies from backstage. Also, Jake seemed to want the gift certificate. Even if I won, my parents would probably not let me use it. He needed it more than I did.

After his nearly getting in trouble for no reason earlier in the week, he deserved a moment of glory. Perhaps a set of nonstick cookware could be his ticket to a life that did not require him to eat gross things for dollars.

This was my chance to do something brave. Something heroic. Like Jason or Harlan.

"Soubise," I said. "S-O-O—"

The bell rang.

Jake practically ran to the microphone, where he spelled the word correctly.

The bee was over.

Jake Wells had won.

34
CHRISSIE

Excerpt from notebook #15:
Principal Floren's breath smells like ketchup.

I couldn't believe it. Jake "Chow" Wells had taken first place.

He was onstage, jumping up and down, looking like he couldn't believe it, either.

As Principal Floren made his way down the aisle, kids in the auditorium began to shout "Chow! Chow! Chow! Chow!" over and over. Jake looked as though he was having the time of his life.

The old ladies, at least, were going to be happy. No one had bet on Jake—his odds were a hundred to one—so they wouldn't have to pay any winners off. It was just as good for them as if Mutual had won.

"Wow!" Principal Floren said, taking the microphone. "I believe this was the most exciting spelling bee we've ever had!"

Principal Floren did not look happy—he looked terrified. I had heard him shouting "No!" when Jennifer missed her word on purpose.

"Who would have thought," Floren continued, "that after all of the terrible rumors and allegations that plagued the bee this year, we would have such a great contest! It's a shame people weren't betting on it!"

My time had come.

"You were!" I shouted from behind the soundboard. "I have proof!"

Everyone turned around and looked at me. I noticed that a lot of the guys with cameras were rushing up to me.

"Chrissie?" asked Floren quietly, looking more frightened than ever. "What are you talking about?"

"You were betting big money on Jennifer to win!" I shouted. "You left the door unlocked so her dad could break in and steal the list! You authorized the break-in, and tried to sabotage Mutual!"

"Lies!" he shouted.

"I have proof!" I shouted back.

I stepped over to the camera that was pointed at the microphone—the one that was being used for the video backdrop showing close-ups of the spellers' faces. I slipped the surveillance recording into the camera, and hit play.

Right away, the image on the screen of Principal Floren standing at the microphone was replaced by an image of him sitting at his desk. I fiddled with the controls on the soundboard to turn up the sound that was coming through the camera.

The image on the screen showed Floren telling Mutual that he thought he deserved a little extra help.

"This is footage of Floren in his office, giving Mutual a copy of the master word list," I shouted. "But the list he gave him wasn't the real list—it was full of misspelled words! I have it right here!"

I held the list up in the air. People gasped. Reporters started moving toward me.

"Wait!" I shouted. "There's more!"

And I took that disc out, and replaced it with the one from the previous Thursday night, now more than a week before. The screen onstage changed to a picture of Floren speaking on the phone.

"This is from the night before the break-in!" I shouted

"Hi, Mitch," the image of Floren on the screen was saying. "Are we still set for . . ." And then the screen turned to fuzz.

"Following this is an eighteen-minute, twenty-second period of blank space," I said. "Principal Floren tried to erase the conversation. But he didn't get the first few seconds! He arranged for Mitchell Van Den Berg to break in and steal the list, so he couldn't be in trouble himself if Jennifer's dad was caught!"

"Lies!" Floren shouted. "I was calling him to set up a golf match! That's all!"

"Why would you erase a conversation about a golf match?" someone shouted.

All the news cameras were now pointing up at Floren.

He stared into the cameras, looking pale and frightened, and didn't say a word.

Mrs. Rosemary immediately jumped up onstage and grabbed the microphone.

"Class dismissed!" she shouted.

Everyone began getting up and running out of the room.

Various playground monitors hustled everyone out of the building—including me—while the news reporters charged the stage, trying to get to Floren.

Outside, the scene was general pandemonium. Lots of kids were trying to break back into the school to see what was going on. Others crowded around Jake, congratulating him on winning the bee.

I fought my way through the crowd around Harlan to talk to him—he was surrounded by people wanting to pat him on the back for his belch—which truly had been a belch to remember. I was proud to have helped.

Before I could get to him, though, I heard Mrs. Boffin behind me.

"Chrissie!" she said. "Congratulations! I KNEW you could do it!"

I was just about to ask what she meant when the reporters caught up with me. They all wanted me to retell the entire story of what had happened and how I knew. And even when I got rid of the reporters, I wanted to start taking depositions from Jennifer, Harlan, Mutual, and everyone else right away. Clearly, my work that day was far from over.

But I was ready.

35
PRINCIPAL FLOREN

expectorate—verb. To cough up and spit out gunk in order to clear one's throat. *It is not considered polite to expectorate at most funerals.*

Well, I screwed it up real good, didn't I?

But, ladies and gentlemen of the school board, what I did, I did for the good of the school. Sometimes you have to bend the rules to keep the school safe. When you're older, Chrissie, you'll understand.

My direct involvement began just after the written test that the students took to qualify for the bee. I had requested that each teacher give me a list of students taking the test, and I myself observed them taking the test after school to gather information. As soon as it ended, I drove to the Burger Baron.

"Welcome to Burger Baron, Principal Floren!" shouted the young man behind the counter. At Burger Baron, they believe that the louder you are, the friendlier you seem, and all employees are taught that the office of principal commands respect.

"Good afternoon," I said. "I'd like the seafood platter."

The young man nodded and pointed toward a door to the side of the counter, and I opened it up and walked in.

As I'm sure you all know, there is no seafood available at the Burger Baron. The little room behind the door was, at the time, home to the main gambling den in Preston, and "seafood platter" was the password to enter.

The gambling den, in fact, is the only reason the Burger Baron is still open at all. The restaurant itself has not turned a profit in years. Few people eat there, and those who do only go once. No one returns for more. Those of you who have tasted the food know why.

A patron seeing the door beside the counter would have assumed that it just led to a storage closet, or possibly an office. Inside, though, was a dim room full of scruffy-looking old men who always appeared to be drunk—which many of them certainly were.

I recognized most of them—at one table sat Wallace Agnew, who had been the janitor at Gordon Liddy until he was fired over that unfortunate incident involving all of that cheese and the poor, poor hamster. After losing his job, he almost never left the Burger Baron.

Ladies and gentlemen of the school board, it's now no secret that I have a problem. Everyone has their vices, and I now admit that mine is gambling. However, I can assure you that I always went to great lengths to make sure no student knew anything about this, lest I become a bad example, and that this was the only time in all my years as principal that I let my problem affect my work as principal in any way. Even then, what I did, I did for the good of the school, as you will soon see.

I will not say that the gambling den at the Burger Baron was a happy place—most of the men at the tables looked as though they had just been in a fistfight, their clothes were largely unwashed, and nobody was smiling or talking. There were no decorations on the bare cement walls, unless you counted the occasional stain. Some of the men would stare blankly at the radio as it broadcast the horse races and football games; others would stare at the wall for hours at a time.

At the end of the room sat Helen Bernowski and Agnes Milhous, the old women who owned the Burger Baron. They were there every day, barely moving from their stools. A few feet away from them sat a large spittoon—when things were slow, as they usually were, they would kill time by making bets as to which of them was a more accurate spitter. It was usually a tie.

When I walked into the room, Helen was hawking a large loogey that landed squarely in the tin spit bucket, making a loud "ping" sound as it hit the metal.

"Ha!" Helen croaked. "Bull's-eye!"

Agnes handed her a wrinkled dollar bill. They usually passed the same dollar back and forth all day.

"Nice shot, Helen," I said.

"Well, well, well," said Helen. "If it isn't the principal!"

"Of course it's the principal, you ninny!" Agnes shouted. "Who else would it be?"

"It's just an expression, you old hag!" shouted Helen.

Besides spitting contests, shouting at each other is Helen and Agnes's favorite activity.

"You got 'em, Principal?" asked Agnes.

"Of course," I said. I walked through the room, carefully avoiding all the globs of spit that had missed the spittoon and ended up on the floor, and handed her a list of every speller, with brief descriptions of them and the odds that they would win the bee.

Most of the time, Helen and Agnes took bets on sporting events that were broadcast over the radio. But the most popular event of the year was the all-school spelling bee at Gordon Liddy Community School—everyone there made bets on it. And, as the students' safety has always been one of my top priorities, I felt that it was my duty to provide all of this information to the local gambling community. If I hadn't, some of the gamblers might have tried to get the information for themselves, putting the students at risk. I did it every year. It was all for the good of the school.

Helen and Agnes looked over the list intently.

"Marianne Cleaver," said Agnes. "It says here she speaks in multiple-choice questions?"

"Yes," I said. "She's one of our best students, but we wonder about her mental health."

"And she has five-to-one odds?"

"Yes."

Five-to-one odds made her the favorite to win—no one else had better odds. Five to one meant that if you bet a dollar on her, Helen and Agnes would pay you five dollars if she won the bee. But no one made bets that small.

"And this Van Den Berg kid is at six to one?"

"Yes," I said. "She doesn't have her sister's level of dedication. Or Marianne's. But I think she's naturally smarter than Marianne."

Agnes nodded.

"What about this kid, Mutual Scrivener? Says here you people think he's some sort of spelling genius, but you gave him ten-to-one odds?"

"He's a bit of a wild card, that Mutual. Today was his first day at Gordon Liddy. We think he's probably a very good speller, but we don't know what sort of study methods he's been using over the years, and we don't have any Iowa Test of Basic Skills scores for him. We wonder if he hasn't had access to the same sort of dictionaries as the other students."

"But you still gave him pretty good odds?" asked Helen.

"Don't tell the man how to do his job!" shouted Agnes. "He's the expert, Helen! And get your chair away from the electrical outlet, or you'll get electrigated!"

"Shut your mouth, Agnes! You'd just love to see me get electrigated!" shouted Helen. "Probably toast a marshmallow off me while I burned up, that's what you'd do! Then you'd have this place all to yourself, and you could use my biscuit recipe and say it was your own!"

"Your biscuits taste like barf!" Agnes shouted. And she leaned her head back and spit out a loogey that landed in the spittoon, narrowly avoiding my head on the way. I should have known better than to stand in the line of fire. Helen handed her back the dollar.

"Nice shot, Agnes," I said.

Agnes smiled. "Well then, Mr. Principal," she said, "who will you be betting on?"

"Oh, you know I never place a bet on the bee," I said. "It wouldn't be appropriate."

"Nonsense!" said Helen. "If a principal does something, that means it's appropriate."

"You weren't thinking of spending a week watching the students, and then making a bet with inside information, were you?" asked Agnes. "Because that would be cheating, Mr. Principal. And you know what happens to cheaters!"

I gulped. In some gambling dens, they break your legs or your thumbs when they catch you cheating. Others just beat you senseless. At the Burger Baron, anyone caught cheating had to clean out the spit bucket.

Nobody, but nobody, ever tried to cheat Helen and Agnes.

"And we really, really think you should be placing a bet this year, Principal."

When Helen and Agnes told you this, they meant that you didn't have a choice. It was an order, and if you refused, they were going to call on you to pay any money that you owed them—and if you couldn't pay, they'd make you go to work at the Burger Baron, washing dishes, until you were paid off.

"All right," I said. "I'll place a bet now."

"Who will it be, then?" asked Helen.

I thought for a moment. My first instinct was to bet on Mutual Scrivener, but that was dangerous. Also, it could be very, very bad for the school if he won. How would it look if a student who had barely spent a day in school did better than students who had been in school their whole lives? No, it was important that Mutual Scrivener not win the bee.

I thought about betting on Jason Keyes, but if he won, people would be suspicious. Marianne had the best odds, but my instincts also told me that all the studying she did could cause her to burn out early. Jennifer seemed like the way to go.

"Van Den Berg," I said. "I'll bet on Jennifer Van Den Berg."

"That's a nice, safe choice," said Agnes. "And goodness knows you need the money, Mr. Principal."

"Because you know what will happen if you don't pay us all the money you owe soon, Floren," said Helen. And she and Agnes both laughed—there are few sounds in the world more terrifying than the sound of them laughing together.

I owed Helen and Agnes thousands of dollars. And if Jennifer lost the bee, or if I refused to make a bet, they would probably make me take a job as a dishwasher at the Burger Baron to pay them back. I might even have to resign as principal to be a full-time dishwasher.

When all the bets were laid, it looked as though Helen and Agnes stood to win the largest amount if Mutual won. I was sure that they would accuse me of cheating if he lost, so I very carefully filmed myself giving Mutual a word list, so it would look like I had actually HELPED the student they wanted to win. They would not have been able to see that the list was full of misspelled words in the recording. I regretted what I was doing to Mutual, of course, but I felt that it was a necessary action on my part. It was important to me, and the school, that Jennifer won, and that Helen and Agnes could not accuse me of cheating.

And that is the real story. My hand was forced.

Thank you, Chrissie, for taking my deposition. I welcome this investigation, because I believe the students have got to know whether their principal is a crook.

Well, I am not a crook.

In all my years as a public servant, I have always tried to do what was best for the school.

36
HARLAN

subligaria—noun. Latin word for underwear. *When the wind blew Caesar's toga around, Roman children would shout, "Clear the street! Clear the area! I see Caesar's subligaria!"*

Ah, it's good to be a legend. I always knew it would be.

I can't even describe how great that belch felt. It's that feeling you get when you've worked really hard to get something, and then you finally get it, and it's everything you thought it would be. And then, if that wasn't a good enough feeling, the place went nuts. I'd even go so far as to say I got more applause than Johnny Dean did when he brought the purple dog onstage.

And right after the bee, people were crowding all around me, congratulating me and wanting me to teach them to burp. I might even have to start up a business giving private burping lessons.

After the crowd died down, one of the guys from the Good Times Gang even came up and started talking to me. He was writing a song about me, he said. Do you believe that? So now every kid at every school the Good Times Gang visits is going to know about me. And that'll spread my fame far and wide for years, you know, because they don't change their routine much at all. Maybe in a hundred or so years they can sing the song at my funeral. In fact, I'll insist on it.

Anyway, I was so caught up in my belching plans that I barely even stopped to think that getting to the top five would take me to districts, too. Maybe I'll even really try my best to come in first there! I let Jake have this one—he wanted it a LOT more than I did, and I'd already done what I planned to do. But who knows? I could probably even make it to nationals, if I study hard enough.

And I realize that there's a lot of talk going around saying that Chrissie gave me the master word list, or at least showed it to me. But she didn't. She told me she had it, but I never looked at it. Never even asked to. It would go against the code of the class clown. I live by the code, and, well, look where it got me!

After all, whenever someone tells me I should steal, or drink, or smoke, or take drugs, or cheat, all I have to do is the same thing I do when the gym teacher tells me to run a lap: Shrug my shoulders and say, "Hey. I don't need to do that stuff. I'm a member of the Good Times Gang!"

37

JENNIFER

honorificabilitudinitatibus—
noun. The condition of being worthy to receive honors. Known for being the longest word used by Shakespeare. *At the end of Bee Day, the best word for the state that Jason, Harlan, Jake, and Mutual were in was honorificabilitudinitatibus.*

I didn't wait for the crowd to die down—the bee was over, and I was going home.

I didn't want to wait around talking to reporters about my dad breaking into the school. I wanted to talk to Mutual a bit, but his parents hustled him into their car the second he was out of the auditorium. So I just started running. I ran all the way home, stopping only to jump into the occasional snowdrift. I hadn't forgotten *all* my priorities.

Maybe I shouldn't have lost the bee. I could have won— I know I could have. But I didn't mind losing to Jake. He wanted it a lot more. I just hoped my parents would understand.

My mother, as usual, was waiting at the door.

"Jennifer!" she shouted when I opened up the door. "Thank goodness!"

"Hi, Mom," I said. "I guess you saw the bee on TV."

"It was brilliant of you," she said. "I always knew you were a genius!"

"Um, Mom?" I asked. "You know I lost, right?"

"That was the brilliant part!" she said. "If you had come in first, when they played that tape showing that Principal Floren helped your dad break in, people would have thought that you were cheating. You proved them all wrong by missing that word—it was a stroke of genius!"

"Yeah," I said. "That's exactly what I had in mind."

"Brilliant," she said again. "Wait till I call Val and tell her!"

Of course that wasn't really what I had in mind, but Mom didn't need to know that.

"And Marianne got creamed!" Mom went on triumphantly. "This is absolutely the best thing that could have happened. You showed that you weren't cheating, you get to go to districts, and Marianne doesn't! Your father will be so proud. You did a very honorable job."

"I'm just glad it's over," I said. "Can I have some hot chocolate? With marshmallow cream?"

"You, Jennifer, deserve all the hot chocolate you want. But it's a long way from over. Districts are only a month away, and you have a lot of studying to do!"

"I suppose so," I said. "And remember how you said that I could drop a couple of activities if I went to districts?"

"Yes." She nodded.

"Well, I think I should probably take some time off from

almost ALL of them. Like, everything but Shakespeare Club."

Mom paused for a minute, and stared at me like I'd just said I was going to quit breathing, just to see what would happen. But then she exhaled, shrugged her shoulders, and tilted her head sideways.

"That may be wise, now that I think about it," she said. "You'll need that time for studying! I'll talk to your father about it."

"You think he'll go for it?" I asked.

"No," she said. "But I'm sure I can reason with him."

"I was sort of afraid he was going to send me to military school if I didn't make it to districts."

Mom sighed. "He's been going on about military school for years," she said. "He even wanted to send Val there. He just wants what's best for you guys, you know. His job isn't really very good, and he wants you and Val to have better ones. Deep down, he knows there are more important things in life than spelling. The spelling bee just makes people go a bit crazy around here."

That had to be the understatement of the year. But it was good to know that she knew Dad was nuts, too.

"You wouldn't let him send me to military school, would you?" I asked.

"Of course not, silly," said Mom. "There's no way he could talk me into it now. Not now that I've seen just how good at sneaking into buildings military school REALLY made him."

A minute later, she brought me a mug of hot chocolate

topped with a whole mountain of marshmallow cream. Hot chocolate had never tasted so good.

Nobody in years to come will really remember who had won the bee—it was Harlan who had been the *real* winner. He had become a hero—twice in one day—and then thrown the bee to let Jake or Mutual have it. And then Mutual, I was sure, had missed on purpose as well. I wasn't entirely sure why he had done that, but it was a really nice thing to do for Jake. And everyone knew that Harlan and Jason had a lot of guts, of course, but doing something like that was probably a huge thing for Mutual. If the rumors about his parents were true, he could probably be kicked out of his family for losing the bee.

I hoped they didn't kick him out. I really wanted to study with him.

I was proud to have spelled with all those guys. And Jason and Brittany and everyone else, too. Everyone but Marianne, of course. But now that the whole thing was over, it was hard to keep feeling all that angry at her. In a weird way, I even felt a little bit sorry for her. But just a little bit.

The all-school bee was over. That was all that mattered to me right then.

A couple of minutes later, I was sitting on my bed, sipping hot chocolate and changing into warm socks. Falstaff was curled up next to me, purring.

And I still had the Shakespeare Club meeting that night to look forward to.

It was going to be a good night.

38
MUTUAL

floccinaucinihilipilification—
noun. The act of estimating something to be worthless. *When it came to the outside world, Mutual's parents were in the habit of floccinaucinihilipilification, but Mutual was seeing things very differently.*

My parents were a little upset that Jake Wells had won the bee, but I told them that I just missed the last word because I was so nervous—I was not used to having so many people watching me, or having so many bright lights on me.

"That is what they do, all right," Mother said, as she drove me home. "I know their tricks and manners! They try to intimidate the children who are not used to the outside world, so their favorite kids have an advantage. But it does not matter too much—you can still come in first in the district bee next month."

The next morning, we drove clear into town so we could buy a local newspaper. The front page headline read FLOREN AUTHORIZED BREAK-IN!

The article said that evidence provided by Chrissie

Woodward proved beyond reasonable doubt that Floren had bet that Jennifer Van Den Berg would win the bee, and it was thought that the eighteen minutes and twenty seconds of footage he had erased would have shown him arranging for her father to break in. Jennifer was not suspected of cheating, since she had not won the bee, anyway, and there was no evidence that she had actually had a copy of the word list.

The article also mentioned that Chrissie had provided the school board with a copy of the sloppy word list Floren had given me, which indicated that he had actually tried to sabotage me—it even had his signature to prove he had written it. So I was in no trouble. My parents were not upset—they only gave me an hour-long lecture to beware of Principal Floren's tricks and manners.

Police officers had arrested the old ladies, Helen and Agnes, who, the paper said, attempted to spit on the officers as they were put into handcuffs. They had then raided the Burger Baron and found a whole den of gamblers in a hidden back room. My parents said that they always knew that the town was full of places like that.

The school board decided to let the results of the spelling bee stand, since it did not appear that any student had actually cheated, but they were launching an investigation into Principal Floren's activities. We called from a telephone in a drugstore to arrange for me to give my deposition.

"I knew it," said my mother. "Gambling! Sabotage! Corruption! What did I tell you, Mutual? The corruption at that school went all the way to the top! It is a wonder nobody was shot!"

"But at least I made it to the district bee," I said. "So I will have to continue attending Gordon Liddy Community School until then."

"Yes," said Mother, scowling. "I suppose you will. But you will have to be a lot more careful. Do not talk to any teachers or even other students, if you can help it. Now you know their tricks and manners, too. I have half a mind to pull you out of there and put you in the Shaker Heights school."

"No," I said. "I would prefer to stay at Gordon Liddy. It would be easier than learning a whole new set of tricks and manners at another school."

"I suppose that makes sense," she said. "You have a lot of studying to do over the next month! You do not need to be all worried about starting over on top of that."

I was more excited by this news than any other. I was happy that I would be competing in the district bee, and happy for Jake, since he had won, and happy that the results would not be contested. But mostly I was excited that I would still be able to attend Gordon Liddy. With Jason and Amber, who were teaching me headbanging skills. And both Jason and Harlan could teach me an awful lot of things that had nothing to do with spelling. And, most importantly, Jennifer was going to be teaching me her method of studying. I would get to spend more time with her. Perhaps just the two of us, alone.

I still had plenty of time to become a famous speller, like Umlaut Eddlebeck and Big John Comma. I was glad to be able to spend another month with Mrs. Boffin's class.

I had a lot to learn.

39

CHRISSIE

Excerpt from notebook #96:
The password to get into the gambling den is "seafood platter."

So there it is. The whole story of the bee, in black and white, as told by the people who lived it.

You no longer have an excuse not to fire Floren.

I still feel terrible about how many kids I got into trouble over nothing over the years. A lot of times, I gave information to the office just hoping that it would get someone some extra help, or a warning, and they ended up getting detention, or missing recess. And I was always a bit disappointed when that happened, but I figured that the people in the office knew best. They made the rules and the decisions, and I always trusted them.

Looking back, I can't believe how stupid I was.

All that time, I was trusting in a low-down, dirty crook.

From now on, things are going to be different. I might still turn Harlan in every now and then, if he does something REALLY bad, but I've come to realize that my real job is to protect the students from the people who run the school.

And that's what I'm going to do. I'm only going to be at Gordon Liddy Community School for a few more months, but in that time, I want to make sure no kid gets in more trouble than he or she deserves. I want to make sure that the place is fair and just to everyone. It sure won't be easy.

But you, dear esteemed members of the school board, can take one easy step and make my job a whole lot easier by firing Principal Floren. I may have lost a lot of trust in your ability to do the right thing, but I still hope you can do it. Even though I still say you stink for not having done it already.

Thank you for your time.

Sincerely,
Chrissie Woodward

APPENDIX:
SELECTED SONGS OF
THE GOOD TIMES GANG

IT'S COOL TO STAY IN SCHOOL
To the tune of "America the Beautiful"

My friends all told me I'd be cool
If I were getting high
I listened and I'm lucky that
I'm even still alive
I thought I'd be an engineer
And sometimes it seems strange
I ended up here on the streets
Just asking for some change!

Chorus

Now I'm a homeless junkie and
I live on crumbs and gruel
'Cause no one ever told me that
It's cool to stay in school.

My shoes are just old boxes and
My hat's a paper bag
I'd tell you just how bad I smell
But I don't like to brag!
There's something growing on my toes
My nostrils really burn
But how to deal with things like that
I had no chance to learn

For I'm a homeless junkie and
I'm dumber than a mule
'Cause no one ever told me that
It's cool to stay in school!

MY AUNT JUDITH SMOKES

My aunt Judith smokes, in fact it's all she ever does
My mom says she's a bum, and that's all she ever was
She watches bad TV all day, and smokes pack after pack
I went to her house one time, and I'm not going back

My aunt Judith could kill you with her breath
One of these days, she's gonna smoke herself to death

Her teeth are always yellow, her fingers always stained
Her voice sounds like a duck that's in an awful lot
of pain
When she says, "Hey, sis, loan me ten bucks" (you see,
she's always broke)
She can't afford to buy much food, it costs too much
to smoke

My aunt Judith could kill you with her breath
One of these days, she's gonna smoke herself to death

Last night Aunt Judith went to bed when she was tired
Her cigarette caught on the bed and set the place on fire
But even at the end, she just had to smoke some more
The firemen said that smoke was rising up from
every pore!

My aunt Judith has breathed her last breath
I always knew that one day, she'd smoke herself to death!

GET HIGH ON SELF-ESTEEM

I don't think there's anything
I can't do anymore
I've been snorting self-esteem
Behind the corner store

Catchy Choreutic Section

You don't need to hallucinate, you only need to dream
All you have to do is get high on self-esteem

When I get full of self-esteem
I feel like such a star
The paparazzi take my picture
While I'm in my car

Chorus

SELF! ESTEEM! SELF! ESTEEM!*

When I think of my future
It's all peaches and cream

---

*This "call and response" section can last anywhere from
thirty seconds to several minutes, depending on how much
time the group needs to kill.

But I might have to go to rehab
'Cause I'm high on self-esteem!

Chorus

IF Y'ALL WANNA JOIN A GANG, JOIN THE GOOD TIMES GANG!

Awwwww yeah!

You might've seen singing groups here before
But you aren't gonna wanna see 'em back anymore
Now that I've been here, boppin' with my crew
We're the Good Times Gang, and we want you!
Everybody knows that we're the best gang around
And as for all the other singing groups in town
We'll take 'em all down, they better not be messin'
With our positive message and our upbeat lessons!
If y'all wanna join a gang, join the Good Times Gang!
If y'all wanna join a gang, join the Good Times Gang!

We pack number two pencils, sharp enough to sting
We have stories to share and songs to sing
So word to your teachers, put your hands in the air
And wave 'em around like you really do care
About being entertained, and learning, too
I know it all sounds too good to be true
But we can do both, with a dose of hysteria
So forget the other gangs in the tricounty area—
If y'all wanna join a gang, join the Good Times Gang!
If y'all wanna join a gang, join the Good Times Gang!

THE BALLAD OF HARLAN STURR*
To the Tune of "The Battle Hymn of the Republic"
("Glory, Glory Hallelujah")

"Is everybody ready?" asked the teacher, looking round.
Our hero bravely answered yes and then he heard
the sound
Of all the students marching to the risers on the floor.
It was the all-school bee!

Chorus

Glory, glory to the class clown! Glory, glory to the class
clown!
Glory, glory to the class clown—the teachers fear
his name!

The spelling bee had finally come, he took his place in line.
He wasn't there to win—no, he had something else
in mind.
An act to make the kids remember him forevermore
There at the all-school bee!

Chorus

He spelled his way correctly through rounds number
four and five.

---

*While some teachers expressed concern that this song did
not contain a "positive message," it quickly became the Good
Times Gang's most popular number.

They got down to the final few, but he was still alive.
His time had come to strike, he laughed about what
was in store
There at the all-school bee!

Chorus

He stepped up to the mike—the time had come to
do or die.
He thought of every test he'd failed, about the grades
gone by,
Then belched into the microphone; the room shook
to its core
There at the all-school bee!

Chorus

The students all were cheering, clapping hands and
stomping shoes.
His comrades all were heard to shout, "A heckuva way
to lose!"
But he spelled the word correctly—what a
suitable encore
For any all-school bee!

Chorus

Thanks to the lovely Ronni, whose support made
this happen. Thanks also to Nadia, my fantastic agent,
and to Stephanie, Kenny, Eleanor,
and everyone at Delacorte Press.

And to Richard Nixon, for being so hilarious.

ADAM SELZER grew up in the suburbs of Des Moines and now lives in downtown Chicago, where he can write in a different coffee shop every day without leaving his neighborhood. Besides working as a tour guide and assistant ghostbuster (really), he moonlights as a rock star.

He is also the author of *How to Get Suspended and Influence People* and *Pirates of the Retail Wasteland*. Check him out at www.adamselzer.com.